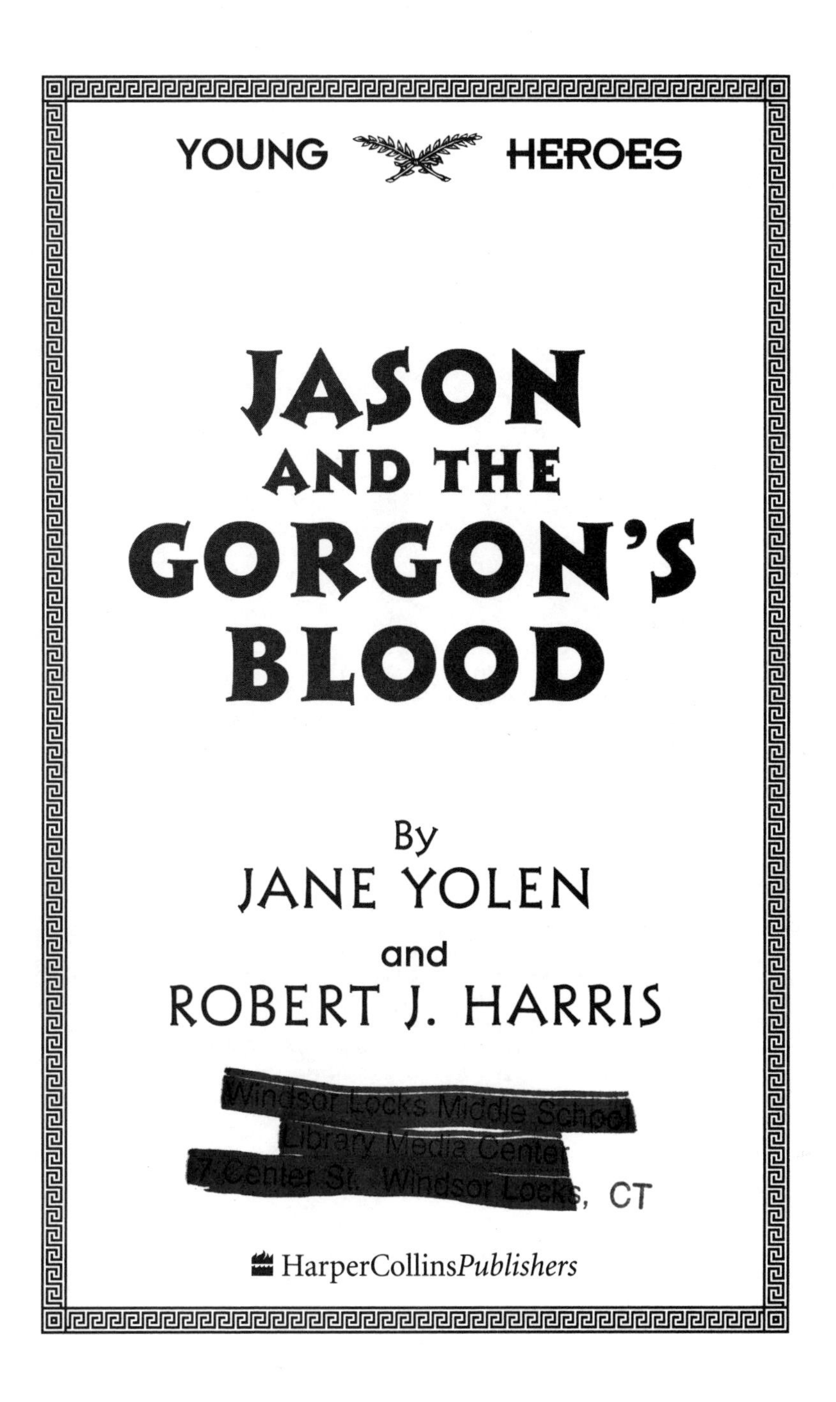

YOUNG HEROES

JASON AND THE GORGON'S BLOOD

By
JANE YOLEN
and
ROBERT J. HARRIS

HarperCollins*Publishers*

Jason and the Gorgon's Blood

Printed in the United States of America. For information address HarperCollins Children's Books, a division of HarperCollins Publishers, 1350 Avenue of the Americas, New York, NY 10019.
www.harperchildrens.com

Library of Congress Cataloging-in-Publication Data
Yolen, Jane.
Jason and the Gorgon's blood / by Jane Yolen and Robert J. Harris.—1st ed.
p. cm. — (Young heroes)
Summary: Jason, who will grow up to become the head of the Argonauts, leads five other boys on a dangerous quest to save the kingdom of Iolcus, learning along the way what it means to be in command.
ISBN 0-06-029452-3 — ISBN 0-06-029453-1 (lib. bdg.)
1. Jason (Greek mythology)—Juvenile fiction. [1. Jason (Greek Mythology)—Fiction. 2. Centaurs—Fiction. 3. Mythology, Greek—Fiction. 4. Adventure and adventurers—Fiction. 5. Heroes—Fiction.] I. Harris, Robert J. II. Title. III. Series.
PZ7.Y78Jas 2004
[Fic]—dc21
2003004096
CIP
AC

Typography by Carla Weise
1 2 3 4 5 6 7 8 9 10
❖
First Edition

JASON AND THE GORGON'S BLOOD

Praise for the previous books
in the Young Heroes series
BY JANE YOLEN AND ROBERT J. HARRIS

ODYSSEUS IN THE SERPENT MAZE

"What was Odysseus like as a teenager? This swashbuckling adventure imagines the epic hero as a 13-year-old who's at once brash, insecure, and wise. The characters are richly drawn, with plenty of girl power to balance the boys' heroics. A page-turner."

—ALA *Booklist*

HIPPOLYTA AND THE CURSE OF THE AMAZONS

"The action is nonstop, fleshed out with accurate details from both history and myth."—*Kirkus Reviews*

ATALANTA AND THE ARCADIAN BEAST

"Another exciting installment in the series will thrill readers. The fast-paced story will engage their imaginations."

—*School Library Journal*

For the Harris boys—
Matthew, Robert, and Jamie—
to take along on all their adventures
—J.Y.

To Alan and Anita,
and Elizabeth and Steven,
some of the original adventurers
—R.J.H.

Contents

CHAPTER ONE

A MATTER OF PIGS

The centaur was angrier than Jason had ever seen him before. He was so angry, he didn't just stamp his hooves and make the earth shake like a drum or roar till all the caves of Mount Pelion echoed with the sound.

No, he was far too angry for that.

He lined up the six boys and paced up and down before them in threatening silence, his hooves padding softly on the grass, his fists clenching and unclenching in a broken rhythm. His unspoken disapproval was like a heavy boulder pressing down on all of them, and Jason most of all.

Especially, Jason thought, *because my mouth is so*

parched and there is a dull throbbing behind my forehead and my limbs ache and I have bumps like small hillocks all over my body. He shook his head to clear it, which just made things worse.

Why can't I remember why I feel this way? Something about the night before. *A revel?* He had never been to a revel before.

"Chiron, master . . ." Prince Acastus began. He always used the centaur's title when he wanted to wheedle his way out of trouble.

But Chiron was not to be cozened. He was simply too angry.

"Silence!" Now he roared, and the sound of his voice shattered a small birch in two.

And my head, Jason thought.

Prince Acastus was smart enough to shut up, moving back behind his cousin Admetus.

Jason wondered who would be the first of the boys to crack. Since Chiron had raised him from infancy, and he was used to the centaur's ways, he knew *he* would not be the one. But these other boys had been on the mountain for only a matter of weeks, sent by their fathers to be trained as hunters, as warriors, as heroes. Sent to the master of all masters, the burly old centaur who was now pacing so angrily before them.

Jason smiled at the thought. As quickly, he stopped smiling. Smiling hurt.

At last the centaur halted in front of them and arched

an accusing eyebrow. Jason hated that look most of all. It signaled some awful punishment was going to follow. And soon.

"Pigs," Chiron said, his voice throbbing and low, like a toothache. "Let us talk about pigs."

The centaur was intimidating enough even when he was not angry. With the body of a wild stallion, all sinewy strength and animal speed, crowned by the torso of a heavily muscled man, he radiated raw power. His bearded face had all the majestic grandeur of the mountain that reared up over their heads.

"I say 'pigs,' and how do you answer?"

Idas, the strongest of the boys, stuck out his chest and set his square jaw in defiance, trying hard to show that he wasn't afraid, but nobody was fooled. They were *all* afraid of Chiron. Centaurs were, after all, bigger and stronger than any human adult. And unpredictable. Though Chiron was different from the rest of his breed. Different, apart—and a master teacher.

Idas' brother, wiry Lynceus, who swore he could spot an ant crawling up a tree trunk clear across the valley, right now had eyes glazed over in panic, as if he'd gone blind.

Tall, gangly Melampus of Pylos had a reputation as a seer. He boasted he could foretell the future by the movements of the birds, and indeed his mind always did seem to be drifting among the clouds. But a single glare from Chiron and he came crashing to earth, taking a nervous step backward.

Admetus didn't even attempt to put on a show. His round, freckled face drooped, and he shuffled his feet nervously.

Behind him Acastus crossed his arms, trying—Jason supposed—to look heroic. *Hard to do*, Jason thought, *while hiding behind someone else.* Acastus kept up the charade for almost five whole seconds before bowing his head under Chiron's relentless gaze.

Will he be merciful? Jason wondered. He knew Chiron had a tender heart under that brawny chest. How often had he seen the centaur stop to tend an injured bird, splinting a broken wing or applying a healing salve.

But do we deserve his mercy? Desperately Jason wished he could remember what it was they had done.

Chiron turned his dark-eyed gaze down to the valley below. "I should have known from the sorry state you were in when you dragged yourselves home last night that you had left some sort of trouble behind you."

"*Home!*" Acastus whispered contemptuously to Admetus, though Jason overheard. "What kind of home is a cave in the side of a mountain?"

Suddenly Chiron passed behind the boys and without warning swerved his massive body. His rump barged into Acastus, knocking the boy flat on his face. The others began laughing, but one glance from Chiron snuffed out their mirth.

"A prince," Chiron said in his teacher voice, "should

be noted for the respect he shows others, not his insolence."

As Acastus clambered to his feet, Jason thought, *He must have forgotten how sharp Chiron's ears are.* For an instant, rebellion flickered in the young prince's eyes. Then he lowered his gaze, fixing his eyes on the ground as he fingered the golden amulet that hung around his neck, a symbol of the royal house of Iolcus.

"Pigs," Chiron said again. "They did not escape their pen without help. Now whose idea was it to set them loose?" He scowled at them, but no one spoke.

"Pigs!" Chiron boomed. Another tree on the edge of the clearing shivered, lost its leaves.

Silence fell again like a smothering blanket.

It was Idas who spoke up at last. "We can't remember," he said sullenly. "Whatever punishment is due, inflict it upon us all equally."

"Idas is right," Lynceus chimed in after his brother. "Except maybe for the part about punishment. If you choose to leave me out, I promise not to complain."

Chiron turned the full force of his eyes upon him. Lynceus seemed to shrivel up as though he were trying to shrink to the size of a dust mote.

"And if setting the pigs free weren't bad enough," the centaur continued, "you decided to climb on their backs and race them through the streets of the village. A terrible sight, I am sure."

Hoi! Jason thought. *So that's what we did!* He was

beginning to remember it now, as if through a haze.

The boys stared down, scuffing the earth with their sandals.

"And the result of this rampage? Three fences knocked down, ten clay pots smashed, a cauldron of soup overturned, chickens set to flight, and women and children terrified out of their wits."

As far as Jason could recall, most of the village children had been laughing at their antics. He could still feel the bruise in the small of his back where he had landed on a rock when his pig threw him off, to gales of laughter and applause. *Surely our escapade wasn't as bad as all that.*

He was about to say so when Chiron added: "Two elders from the village visited me this morning while you were still sleeping off your folly. They wanted to flog you in the village square."

"Flog us!" Acastus blurted out. "Admetus and I are princes."

Chiron looked at him under beetling brows. "I persuaded them to leave your punishment to me."

The boys let their collective gaze fall on Jason, as if begging him to say which would be worse—the flogging or Chiron's choice.

"I had to give them one of my best goats and five jars of honey by way of compensation," Chiron added.

Jason winced. He'd been on good terms with the people of the village and could always count on them for something to eat and drink when he was running an errand for Chiron. Now he wondered if he could ever go back there.

"So whose notion was this barbaric race?" Chiron demanded.

Like water gushing from a smashed jar, the boys all started talking at once.

"Somebody said something about the S-Scythians and the Amazons," Admetus stammered.

"Yes, about how they ride on the backs of horses instead of using chariots like civilized folk," Lynceus added.

"It seemed like a test of skill," Melampus finished lamely, "at the time."

Jason cleared his throat. "The truth is, master," he said, "we're not sure whose idea it was. I . . . we don't remember it very well. Except"—he rubbed his back—"some of the bumps."

Chiron nodded somberly. "Yes, I can believe that. And why?"

The boys were silent again.

"Because of the wine." The centaur's mouth curled around the final word as if it were distasteful.

Hoi, Jason thought, *the wine!* He'd never had any wine before. And now he couldn't even remember what it tasted like.

"The jar was lying unattended," said Acastus.

"We left two rabbits we'd killed to pay for it," Admetus added.

"Rabbits I shot," bragged Idas.

"You missed the second one," Jason reminded him. "I shot that one."

"I wounded it," said Idas, "leaving you an easy target."

"Enough!" Melampus complained, clutching his skull. "You're making my head hurt all over again."

"Was that *all* you caught?" Chiron asked disdainfully. "Two small rabbits? You were supposed to be on a hunting expedition."

"We got close to a deer," said Idas.

"But there was a big argument over who should fire the first shot," said Lynceus. "The noise scared it off."

Jason remembered that part. And how no one would listen to him when he warned them to be quiet. How they laughed at him. How they called him Mountain Boy and Chiron's Slave.

"So," Chiron concluded solemnly, "instead of carrying on with the hunt, you got drunk on wine and behaved like barbarians."

"You never let us have any wine," said Idas sullenly. "Is it any wonder that it goes to our heads once we drink some?"

"At my father's palace I can drink all the wine I want," said Acastus.

"Let your father teach you to drink wine, then," said Chiron. "My task is to teach you to be strong adults, to hunt like a man, to be a virtuous hero."

All down the line noses wrinkled at the word, except for Jason. He alone nodded. *Yes*, he thought, *that's what Chiron always says.*

"A virtuous hero," Chiron repeated. "And how can you remember what is virtuous or honorable when you cannot think straight?" He tapped himself on the forehead to emphasize the point.

"Do you mean a virtuous man cannot drink wine?" Idas asked.

"A virtuous man knows when to drink and when not to," Chiron answered gravely. "He knows when it is appropriate to celebrate a victory or toast the gods, but he also knows when wine will lead to disgrace. One day you may know this, too, but until that time, I forbid wine to all of you."

Melampus rubbed his brow. "That doesn't help my head right now," he complained.

"I have a cure for that," said Chiron. "However, before I can brew it, you will have to fetch special herbs from the valley of Daphnis."

"What—*all* of us?" Acastus exclaimed. "Why not just send Jason?" He said it with a straight face. "He'll be swiftest. And surely swiftness under these circumstances is a virtue."

Jason gave him a sidelong look that was as sharp as a dagger but bit back any other response.

Chiron observed his restraint and gave Jason a barely perceptible nod of approval. "As you have been partners in folly," he said, "so you will be partners in the cure. I will need eyebright, pennyroyal, feverfew, and—rarest of all—bawme. So the more of you there are to search, the quicker you will be. If you set out now, you can be back by sundown."

He began chivvying the boys down the slope, and they complained loudly because of their hurting heads and aching limbs.

"Do you mean us to go without weapons?" Idas was aghast.

"Weapons are for warriors and hunters," said Chiron icily. "You have proven yourselves to be neither." He stomped his feet. "The weapons will remain in the back of my cave until you are ready for them."

"But if we can't hunt, what will we have to eat?" Melampus asked.

"There are wild fruits and berries aplenty," replied the centaur, waving at them with a dismissive hand.

"But suppose we run into trouble?" asked Admetus.

"That is the very point I am trying to make," said Chiron. "For once in your thoughtless lives, I expect you to avoid trouble."

"That's fine as long as trouble avoids us, too," Lynceus murmured.

Melampus trudged up to the centaur and pleaded, "Could we at least take some water?"

Chiron leaned his bearded face close to the boy. "No, Melampus, you cannot. This is supposed to be a punishment. Though I suppose you could go into town and beg for the flogging instead." He waved them away but signaled Jason to hang back.

Reluctantly, Jason remained as the others trudged downhill.

The old centaur's face grew thoughtful. "I am disappointed in you, Jason," he said as soon as the others were out of hearing. "Those boys were sent here to be trained precisely because they are so undisciplined, but you are not. I have raised you myself. I expected better."

"I just want to be one of them," Jason said. He hated that his eyes were tearing up. "For the first weeks they would hardly speak to me, treating me like a servant. Last night was the first time—"

"Better you be thought a servant than a fool."

"If a person is of royal blood, he can be a fool and no one will ever dare call him one," said Jason bitterly. "But I'm only an orphan, so people can call me anything they like."

A curious expression flickered in Chiron's wise eyes, and his voice softened. "Is that all you think of yourself? A worthless orphan? Have I not taught you to take pride in your skills and talents?"

Jason turned away to hide the misery in his face. "What use are those skills and talents if I spend all my days here tending goats and growing vegetables? There's nothing heroic in that. Or virtuous either."

"A time will come when you will need everything I

have taught you," Chiron assured him. "More than that I cannot say."

Jason felt the old centaur's familiar, reassuring hand rest on his shoulder, but for the first time in his life it didn't help. He shrugged it away.

"You'd best hurry after them," the centaur said, removing his hand, "before they get irretrievably lost."

CHAPTER TWO

THE WILD BAND

Jason bounded down the slope after the other boys, his long blond hair flying about his face. "Hold up! Wait for me!"

Melampus stopped and looked back. "Here he comes, nimble as a goat."

"Yes, and almost as clean," Lynceus said.

"What kept you?" Admetus asked as Jason arrived, puffing, in their midst. "Has Chiron been giving you last-minute instructions?"

"Like don't get into trouble," Idas mocked.

"And be sure to be back by sunset," said Melampus, imitating the centaur's deep voice.

Lynceus sneered. "And remember to wash behind your ears." He stuck out his tongue.

"He was probably told to spy on us," said Acastus, "so that he can bring back a lot of tales to his master."

"I'm no spy!" Jason declared hotly. "I'm as much under Chiron's discipline as you are."

"Well, it's a bit different for you, isn't it?" said Acastus witheringly. "You aren't used to anything better." He turned his back on Jason and started on down the mountainside.

Jason understood that they were all taking their aching heads and humiliation out on him. He understood—but that didn't make it any easier to bear, so he stayed well to the rear of them the rest of the way. After all, in a few days' time, these well-bred pupils of Chiron's were due to return home to their families. But Jason had no family and no home other than Chiron and the cave.

The valley of Daphnis was on the far side of Mount Pelion, and the trek took them a long way from the village, just as Chiron had intended.

They walked for about an hour before stopping at a stream Jason knew of. It was icy cold, for it came tumbling down from the snowcapped heights of the mountain. After the long hike, the water was especially sweet; the shock of it first in their cupped hands, then in the mouth, was delicious.

"Look, I'm going to stop here and take a nap," said Acastus, wiping his palms on his tunic. "I'll meet up with you all on the way back."

"Who said you were exempt from Chiron's orders?" Admetus challenged him.

"Don't you think you can manage without me?" Acastus smiled slowly.

"That's not the point." Admetus' homely face was stern and his lips were set together in a hard, thin line.

Fearing a fight, Jason said quickly, "Chiron expects us to work together."

"He probably expects to live forever, too, but that's not going to happen, is it?" Acastus retorted. "This moss over here looks too soft and comfortable to pass up."

"I think you should come along," Idas said very deliberately. "I don't see why the rest of us should do all the work." Hands on hips, Idas was like a small mountain, and not—in Jason's opinion—someone to make mad.

Acastus gave him a big grin and shrugged. "You can take a nap, too, if you like. Four is more than enough for this little errand. Especially with goat boy to lead the way."

"I think we should *all* go," said Idas, glowering at the prince.

"Idas is right," put in Lynceus. "We wouldn't want to leave anyone behind. Besides, who knows what dangers might be lurking around here?" He looked over his shoulder as if that danger were right behind him.

Acastus shrugged again and held up his hands. "Well, if you all insist, I guess I'll forget about my nap. After all, I *am* your leader."

"Some leader," Admetus muttered, though only Jason heard him.

They all bent for one last drink of the cold mountain water and then, following Acastus, continued along the mountain path.

The valley of Daphnis was crisscrossed with many tiny rivulets, most no more than a trickle or a boggy spot, for it was high summer now and the smaller streams had dried up. Still, the valley was one of the most fertile areas for miles and so a good place to gather plants and herbs.

While the others knelt on the ground, plucking bits of possible greenery, Acastus perched himself on a rock and rested his chin on his fist, humming some bright tunes. All the while he toyed with his amulet. It was molded in the shape of a stag's head, with finely wrought antlers and red eyes cut from rubies. More than once Acastus had told the other boys how his father had given him this royal symbol so that, even when he was living rough on Chiron's mountain, he would always remember that he was a prince.

As if he lets us forget that for a moment, Jason told himself. Acastus was a braggart who held his rank above his head as if it were a tent to keep him from all ills. *Ignore him.* Jason knew that if he wanted to become friends with the others, he'd have to accept Acastus, too. Despite his boasting, Acastus really was the group's head, for his rank as prince of the great city of Iolcus was the highest of them all.

For an hour Jason was able to do just that—ignore Acastus, who made a point of lolling about. Most of Jason's time was spent teaching the others which green sprigs were herbs and which were weeds or—worse—which were poisonous. He showed them bawme, with its dark, squarish leaves, and feverfew, which usually grew by low hedges.

Melampus already knew most of the herbs, though even he did not know bawme, which could only be found in really wild places. The other boys had to be watched constantly, for they seemed incapable of remembering for more than a moment the difference between herbs and weeds.

The worst was Acastus, who didn't pick a single thing nor move from his perch. Finally Jason could stand no more. Striding over to the rock, he stood right in front of the prince.

"I suppose you expect even tiny plants to come running in answer to your royal decree," he said. He could feel the heat rising to his cheeks.

"What a strange idea," said Acastus, raising an eyebrow, "that plants should come running." He laughed. "Have you been at the wine again, Jason?" He tutted disapprovingly. "No virtue in that, you know."

"Well, what do you think you're doing?" Jason persisted.

Acastus put his head back on his hands in an exaggerated manner, as if giving this much thought. Then he looked up and yawned. "I'm working out our route back to the cave. The way you brought us was far too long and arduous; too many boulders. There must be an easier way."

The other boys had all stopped their work and were listening to the exchange, their hands full of greenery.

"There's going to be a fight," Lynceus said.

"Good," said Idas. "I was getting bored. I bet you that onyx necklace of yours that Acastus wins."

"And what do I get if I win the bet?" Lynceus asked.

"You get to keep your onyx necklace."

"I think Jason will win," said Admetus.

The others laughed.

"And those pigs we rode last night will sprout wings and fly," Lynceus said. "Acastus has him in both weight and height."

Jason barely heard this exchange, for he was fully concentrating on Acastus, who seemed determined to bait him.

"Surely," Jason said slowly, "you can think and gather herbs at the same time."

Acastus stretched his arms and straightened his back. "When we get back, you can tell Chiron what a bad boy I've been," he drawled.

"I won't tell him anything," said Jason. "I'm not a tell-all." *There, that should do it. Now we can both claim victory.*

But then he added, "Still, I expect you to do your share."

"*You* expect?" Acastus laughed. "And who are you? A peasant boy whose parents threw him out to make room for more goats."

That was so close to what Jason feared, he shot back without thinking. "And what did *your* father throw you out for?"

This obviously hit too close to the bone. Acastus jumped to his feet and shoved Jason backward with both hands. Jason staggered and only narrowly avoided tumbling into a pricker bush.

"If Chiron is such a wise teacher, he should have taught you to know your place, Goat Boy. Be careful what you say to princes. Don't raise your voice to them, don't talk back to them, and never . . . *never* . . . presume." Acastus' face blazed red. "If this were my father's palace, you'd be whipped for saying such a thing."

Hoi, Jason thought, *and what a sore spot that is!* He suddenly realized that another word on the matter and he would provoke Acastus beyond any kind of apology. Then a fight between them would be inevitable. Chiron had warned him repeatedly that the virtuous man does not fight unless there is no other choice. And while Jason knew he could probably hold his own in a fight with Acastus—despite the prince's greater height and weight—he immediately lowered his voice. "Do what you like, Prince Acastus. We need to be finished here before it gets dark."

He turned to rejoin the others as they finished gathering the herbs.

"So you're afraid of the dark as well," said Acastus, his voice like a sting.

Jason felt his fingers curl into fists, all of Chiron's words of wisdom drowned out by the drumbeat pounding in his head.

"What's that?" Admetus exclaimed suddenly.

In the distance Jason could hear an ominous rumble. So the drumbeat wasn't just in his head.

"Is it thunder?" Melampus rubbed his brow and squinted at the sky.

Admetus looked up as well. "No, the sky is clear."

"It sounds like horses," said Idas.

"Idas is right," said Lynceus. "Maybe it's chariots."

Acastus kicked a stone. "That would be just our luck, running into a raiding party of Thracian charioteers. May the gods curse Chiron for sending us out here in the middle of nowhere without our weapons!"

"A lot of use weapons would do the six of us against a Thracian war band," said Admetus.

Jason listened carefully to the sound. He knew he'd heard it before. Then he had it. Turning to the others, he said, "That's not thunder or horses or a war band of charioteers. It's something much worse."

"What are you talking about, Goat Boy?" snapped Acastus.

Before Jason could answer, Lynceus was pointing to a

cloud of dust at the far end of the valley. "There!"

"What is it?" Idas demanded. "What do you see?"

Lynceus strained his sharp eyes to identify the forms emerging from the dust. "Horses," he said.

"Hah!" That was Idas.

"But I see men as well."

"Chariots, then," said Admetus.

Lynceus shook his head. "No, Jason is right. It's something else."

By now they could all see what was approaching—a band of centaurs, a dozen of them at least, their long hair flying as they galloped down the valley.

"What do you think they want?" Melampus asked.

"Maybe to lecture us on knowledge and virtue," drawled Acastus.

"These centaurs aren't like Chiron," Jason warned. "They're wild."

"A bit like us," Lynceus joked, "except with twice as many legs."

Before anyone could laugh at his joke, the centaurs were in the clearing, brandishing wooden clubs over their heads and whooping ferociously, heading straight for the boys.

Jason recognized the leader. His name was Nessus, and about a year before, he'd staggered into Chiron's cave, his flank ripped open by the spear of a Thessalian hunter. Pale and shaking, he'd collapsed on the floor before Chiron could catch him. In spite of the awful wound, Chiron had cured him, and Nessus had left a few days later. *And without a single word of gratitude*, Jason recalled.

Nessus wore what looked worryingly like a human skull suspended from a leather cord around his neck. The others sported necklaces and bracelets made from bones, claws, and horns. They'd painted the human parts of their bodies with streaks of dark blue and bloodred, which gave them a savage, warlike appearance.

"Not like us at all," Jason told the boys quickly. "Chiron calls them a 'rough and careless breed.' They live on raw meat, are usually drunk, and filled with rage. Chiron says they fight all the time, even among themselves."

"They do look dangerous," Admetus whispered.

"They *are* dangerous," Jason said. "Chiron told me they kill humans who annoy them. He said that if I see any of them to just get out of the way."

"Then why are we just standing here?" Acastus demanded. "We need to get to a spot we can defend." He started toward a cluster of rocks, waving to the others to follow.

"No, this way!" shouted Admetus, dashing toward a stream. "The water will slow them down."

Melampus started to follow him, then hesitated, torn between the two princes.

"Stop!" Jason cried. "We have to stay together."

But it was too late. Idas and Lynceus had already

bolted off in a third direction of their own.

At the sight of the boys fleeing, the centaurs redoubled their whoops and galloped even faster to intercept them. Two with dappled bodies pulled ahead of Acastus before he could reach the rocks. He stumbled back, arms shielding his head as the centaurs trotted around him, shaking their clubs.

Another centaur, with a long gray tail, caught up with Admetus and cuffed him on the back of the head, knocking him flat. Admetus scrambled desperately away, got up, and staggered back toward Jason.

The two brothers were cut off as well, by a trio of dark-bodied centaurs who herded them toward the rest.

"You didn't even try to get away," Acastus said, sneering at Jason.

"I stood my ground," Jason retorted. "All you did was give them some sport. And showed them how weak we are."

Now the centaurs had formed a loose circle around them and were whirling their weapons in the air. Occasionally one would rise up on his back legs, front feet pawing the air. They shouted back and forth to one another, mocking the boys with their neighing laughter.

The boys pressed together, back to back, as the centaurs drew closer.

"What do we do now?" Acastus whispered to Jason.

"I wish I knew," Jason said, his voice cracking on the final word.

CHAPTER THREE

BAD OMENS

The big centaur Nessus fixed Jason with a contemptuous glare. "Look, here's Chiron's pet boy."

"So, are you *all* pupils of the good and wise Chiron?" sneered a centaur to his right, whose eyebrows met in the middle, which only added to his bestial appearance.

"What are you doing out here in the wild? Hunting monsters?" cried a third. His horse body was spotted, as if with some terrible disease. "Perhaps you've found them!" He beat his fists on his chest.

All of the centaurs seemed to think this was outrageously clever, and they laughed loudly.

"But wait!" said Nessus. "They have no weapons.

What's the matter, little warriors? Forget your swords and spears?"

"We'll have them next time!" Acastus burst out.

Jason wanted to knock him flat for being so stupid. The last thing they wanted to do was antagonize the centaurs. He stepped forward. "Chiron sent us to fetch herbs for a healing draught," he said quickly. "We're not hunting." He held up empty hands. "As you noted—we have no weapons."

"A huntsman once tried to kill me!" Nessus roared in sudden anger. "Tore me up with his spear. But I survived."

The other centaurs applauded and several laughed again, a long neighing sound.

"Yes, I remember," Jason began in a soft voice. "I helped Chiron heal—"

Nessus did not hear, or deliberately wished not to hear, interrupting Jason. "I tracked him down later. He claimed when he threw his spear he thought he was aiming at a deer. A deer!"

The centaurs laughed and called to one another: "A deer! He thought Nessus was a deer!"

"Well, he won't be hunting deer again," Nessus shouted above them, "because I cracked his skull open—like this!" He lashed out with his club, and Jason had to duck to keep his own head from being smashed.

The others centaurs apparently thought this looked like fun, for they lunged forward, swinging at the boys with their clubs. The boys had to duck and dodge for all they were worth, and still some of them took blows to the back or shoulder.

Finally the centaurs were laughing so hard they had to stop their game so they could catch their breath.

Admetus, who had taken at least one blow—for his shoulder was already purpling—whispered to Jason, "We could make a dash for it. Maybe some of us could get away."

"You tried that already," Jason reminded him. "There's nothing the centaurs like better than chasing running prey."

"So what do you suggest?" Acastus snapped. "That we just stand here and take more blows?"

"Yes," Jason answered firmly, "if we have to. Stand here until they get bored. They're not really very bright and they'll leave soon, as long as we don't provoke them."

"They don't look bored to me," Lynceus muttered, nodding his head at the centaurs, who were still laughing and slapping their hands together.

Just then the centaurs all looked up.

"Look at them, Nessus! Not much sport here," called out the spotty centaur.

Another pointed at Idas. "That one at least seems big enough for a fighter," he said. "But I doubt he has the spirit." He trotted over to Idas, presented his rear to the boy, and whipped his tail across Idas' face.

Idas clenched his fists and started forward.

"Don't move," Jason warned.

Idas clenched his jaw and stood his ground, though there were welts across his cheek where the tail had struck him.

"These are women, not warriors," Nessus agreed. "Let's go . . . and leave them to their pretty flowers."

"There's still some fun to be had," cried a centaur who wore a necklace of bear claws around his neck. "Let's chase them across the valley and *then* hunt them."

Nessus walked over unhurriedly and grabbed hold of the bear-claw necklace, twisting it so tightly it choked the centaur till his face turned purple. "Have you forgotten what we're really after, Hylaus?"

Hylaus raised a hand, signaling his obedience, and Nessus released him. Then, lofting his club high above his head, Nessus galloped off across the meadow and into the trees. The others followed, shouting and whistling and waving their clubs.

Idas picked up a rock and was about to throw it after them, but Acastus grabbed his wrist and held him back. "There'll be another time," he promised through gritted teeth. "Another time when we're armed. With bows as well as swords. Let that rabble try us then!"

The boys shouted their agreement.

"For now can we finish what we came here for?" asked Jason.

Halfheartedly, the boys returned to their work. Even Acastus helped to gather some herbs. It was as if the meeting with the wild centaurs had given him some sense of comradeship with the others.

By the time they had filled all the herb bags, the sun was sinking to the west beyond the Bay of Thessaly and Acastus' city of Iolcus.

"Maybe we should find someplace to sleep for the night," said Lynceus, stifling a yawn. "Chiron is probably still mad at us anyway."

"If we don't go back he'll be even madder," said Jason.

"We could just not go back at all," Acastus suggested.

"That's very well for you, Acastus. Your home is just down there." Lynceus waved a hand vaguely toward the west. "But some of us have a long way to travel, and we'd have to do it without food or drink or weapons or coins."

"Hold on," said Admetus. "Look at Melampus."

The gangly Melampus was standing up straight and staring fixedly at the sky. He'd gone as rigid as a spear shaft.

"What is it, Melampus?" Jason asked. "What's the matter?"

Melampus pointed to a flock of birds wheeling across the sky, filling the air with their piercing cries.

"They're upset," he said. His brow wrinkled in

concentration. "They're speaking about Chiron."

"Oh, he's not listening to the birds again, is he?" Idas groaned. "I swear the gods stole his wits when he was in the cradle. I mean, who can believe that story about the grateful snakes?"

"What story?" Jason asked.

"You must have slept through it, Goat Boy," Acastus said with a sneer. "He's told the rest of us often enough."

"But I don't know . . ." Jason began before Idas interrupted him.

"Well, Melampus claims that as an infant he helped some snakes and they licked his ears and after that he could understand the language of animals."

"I can believe that," Jason said quietly. "He's very good."

"And I," Admetus said.

Acastus laughed. "If you believe that rubbish, you're as mad as he."

Melampus hissed and waved his hand irritably for silence. "Let me listen!"

"Listen away if you will, but I'll tell you what they're saying: 'Worms, flies, barley seed,'" Acastus said in a high-pitched voice. "They're saying: 'Hawks, owls, foxes, look out!'"

"No, they're not," Melampus said. "They're saying there's been trouble . . . a fight . . . in Chiron's cave. They're saying that if we knew any better, we'd be heading right back there now."

Jason grabbed Melampus by the arm. "What about Chiron? What are they saying about Chiron?"

Melampus shook his shaggy head. "I don't know. They've gone silent."

"Convenient." Acastus gave a short, sharp bark of a laugh, but the boys were no longer paying any attention to him.

"Do you think those centaurs we met had anything to do with the fight?" Admetus asked.

The boys looked at one another fearfully, for Chiron—much as they begrudged his hard ways—was their teacher.

Finally Admetus said, "Surely they wouldn't hurt a fellow centaur."

Jason shook his head. "He may be of the same race, but he's nothing like them."

"Oh, this is *stupid*," said Acastus. "Some birds start twittering overhead and you all panic as if Pan's pipes were ringing in your ears."

"Melampus has been right before," Lynceus pointed out. "Remember when he warned us about that storm."

"The skies were warning enough," Acastus replied, both hands held up in exasperation.

"And there was the time he convinced that mouse to find my lost ring," said Admetus.

"He probably dropped it himself so he knew where to look," Acastus said. "Ignore him."

"Are you calling me a thief?" Melampus' face was

beginning to purple in anger.

"I'm saying there are many explanations for what happened," Acastus answered. "And understanding the speech of animals is the least of such explanations." He turned to the others. "So I say again, ignore him."

"We can't afford to ignore him, if there's even the slightest chance Chiron needs our help," Jason said. "We have to get back to the cave as fast as we can." He started across the meadow at a lope, thinking that Chiron was not only his teacher, he was the only real friend—the only family—he had in all the world. And even if the other boys didn't want to come along, he'd go without them.

He'd gotten halfway across the meadow when Melampus caught up.

"Jason, wait!" he cried, his voice coming out in spurts. "It's getting dark! You have to help us find the way back. We'll never make it without you."

Jason paused and chewed his lip in frustration. Chiron would have said never to abandon the others, no matter what his hurry.

"All right, but we have to move quickly," Jason called back, and waited till they all caught up.

By the time the cave mouth came into sight, they had only the stars and a half-moon to light their way.

"Stay here," Jason said. "Let me see if there's anything wrong." He already knew something was not right, had known it from the moment he'd realized the cave was unlit. There was no fire, not even a torch burning in the holder. In all the years he'd been with the old centaur, the lights had never gone out completely.

He'd realized that same moment that the safest thing was for him to go on alone. His stomach wasn't happy about that; it felt cold and heavy. His cheeks went red-hot. But he didn't dare risk all their lives.

When he got to the entrance, he was forced to halt because the cave was pitch-black and he had to feel his way inside.

"Chiron?" he called softly. "Chiron, are you there?" Then he was silent, listening. He heard a low, ragged breathing coming from somewhere inside. As his eyes adjusted to the gloom, he could just make out the shapes of the centaur's spare furnishings: some tables, cooking pots, a pair of barrels. And there beyond them, a crumpled form lay on the straw-covered floor.

Jason darted forward, tripping on the way, and fell on his knees at Chiron's side. Running his hand over the centaur's head, neck, torso, he came at last to the bulk of the horse body. He put his head down onto the torso and could feel the labored breaths passing like tremors down that mighty frame.

At least he is alive, Jason thought, and aloud whispered, "Chiron, can you hear me?"

A long, drawn-out rasp was the only reply.

Something made a scratching sound behind him,

and he looked over his shoulder just as a sudden light flared. Melampus had struck a pair of flints and sparked the kindling heaped up inside the circular stone hearth. Quickly the flames gained strength, bringing a much-needed warmth to the cave and casting a flickering illumination over the stricken centaur.

Jason was horrified. Chiron's face and arms were dappled with livid bruises and one of his legs seemed bent at an unnatural angle.

Sweeping Chiron's long hair back from his brow, Jason saw that the old centaur's eyes were firmly shut and blood had dried around the sides of his mouth.

The boys crowded into the cave, lending Chiron more warmth but fast using up the air. For a second Jason thought to throw them all out, then reconsidered. They needed to see, to understand.

"Is he alive?" Acastus asked, voicing the fear for them all.

Jason bit his lower lip. "Yes. But only just."

CHAPTER FOUR

THE HIDING PLACE

The boys quickly covered the old centaur with a woolen blanket and put a sackcloth stuffed with straw under his head. Melampus tore strips of linen to make bandages and, with a long stick, set Chiron's front leg.

Carefully they fed Chiron a warm broth cooked over the now-roaring fire. They couldn't move him onto his straw bed, for he was much too heavy, but instead brought the bed to him, rolling him onto his side and tucking the straw under him.

In the light of the fire they could see the marks of fists and hooves on his body, so purple that the human part was almost as dark-colored as the horse part.

"Jason, go to Chiron's cupboard and get me some

mint and angelica—tops and seeds—plus wormwood, oil of juniper, and . . ." Melampus put his finger to his head as if that could aid memory. "And rosemary."

Leaping up, Jason took a branch from the hearth fire. He lit the taper in the little bronze oil lamp that had been overturned in the fight. Then he went back into the drying alcove where Chiron kept his herbs. Quickly gathering the ones Melampus had asked for, he returned with them clutched in his hand.

"Ground together," Melampus was telling the others, "and mixed with fresh spring water and spirits, they will make a salve for his cuts and bruises."

"How do you know all that?" Idas asked.

"I worked with my old nanny to heal the little snakes who—"

"Yes, yes," Acastus said in disgust, "the little snakes who licked your ears and taught you animal speech. Well, in case you hadn't noticed, Chiron is no little snake." He stood up and went to the entrance to the cave. The moon and stars now being hidden behind clouds, he could see nothing in the impenetrable dark. So he simply stood, one hand on his spear, gazing out and trembling slightly.

Meanwhile, deep inside the cave, Melampus mixed and spread the salve. Then, sighing, he stood. "There's no more we can do until the old man wakes."

"If he wakes," said Admetus.

"Of course he'll wake! How can you say such a

thing?" Jason was taken aback by how shrill his own voice sounded.

"Admetus only says what we're all thinking," said Melampus.

"Don't blame the messenger. The rest is in the hands of the Fates."

"Then we'd all better get some sleep," Idas said, yawning.

"You can go back to your own cave," said Jason. "I'll stay here with Chiron." It was his way of apologizing.

"Perhaps I'd better stay, too," said Melampus.

"You've already done all you can," Jason reminded him. "I'll fetch you if he needs you."

Melampus raised an eyebrow at the brusqueness of Jason's tone.

"We can all stay a bit longer," said Admetus. "I know that I—for one—don't feel much like sleeping."

The others quickly agreed.

In fact, none of them could sleep. Instead they squatted by the fire and discussed what must have happened.

"It was those centaurs!" said Idas, smacking a fist into the palm of his hand.

"Of *course* it was those centaurs," Acastus said, leaving his post by the cave door. "No one else could have inflicted such wounds."

"I'll bet Chiron put up a fight," Lynceus added.

"He would have been magnificent," Melampus said.

Admetus shook his head. "It's amazing they didn't kill him."

"Not for want of trying," Jason called to them, for he'd been listening to the conversation from his place by Chiron's side.

"Well, it's his own fault," Acastus said, shaking his head. "If he hadn't sent us off on that fool's errand, this wouldn't have happened."

"If only we hadn't ridden the pigs . . ." Admetus began, then stopped when the others glared at him.

"What could *we* have done to stop the centaurs?" Idas asked. "You saw how big and wild they were."

"At least we would have had our weapons here." Acastus sounded angry and bitter, but there was something else underneath his anger. It took Jason a minute to figure it out, and then he had it. The prince was frightened.

I wonder why? Jason thought before turning back to Chiron and putting a hand on the old centaur's cheek. He was cool, but not cold.

The boys talked wearily for another few minutes before getting up and walking outside to their own, smaller cave, where their straw pallets and blankets awaited them. But they were each careful to collect a weapon first.

Jason knew he'd been curt with them all, especially with Melampus, who deserved better for his help, and

Admetus, who had at least tried to place the blame where it truly belonged. But Jason didn't have the heart to talk to them now. He wanted to be left alone with Chiron, his foster father, his teacher, his friend.

More than that, something had been nagging at the back of his mind. He'd been trying to figure out what had driven Nessus and the centaurs to this particular violence, and a possible answer had occurred to him.

Before telling the others, he needed to check it out. Taking the little bronze oil lamp, he pressed deep into the cave, past the chests and cupboards in which Chiron stored his possessions, all the way to the solid wall at the back. He remembered the first time he'd explored this wall, imagining that there might be a secret way through it into the heart of the mountain. He'd been about eight years old and alone, for Chiron had gone down into the valley on some errand. By sheer chance he had happened upon a hinged section of rock that swung open when he pressed against it. It exposed an alcove, two feet high.

Bending down now with the lamp, he found it again, the secret doorway, only this time it was lying wide open. He stretched an arm into the dark alcove and felt all around.

The alcove was empty.

There had been two clay jars in there before. A red one and a blue one.

When Chiron had found him on that earlier occasion,

Jason had been trying to pry the lid off one of the jars. The centaur had snatched it away with a mixture of anger and fear. "Never, never, never touch those jars again, boy," Chiron had shouted. "Swear this on your life."

Eight years old and he'd sworn the oath. Had kept it, too, till this very moment.

"And swear you'll never speak of this to a soul."

That was easier. Who did Jason at age eight know but the old centaur? He'd sworn that, too.

But when Jason had asked innocently what was in the jars, Chiron's face had become as dark as a storm cloud. "Do not even think about asking," the centaur had ordered.

Is it too late now to find out the secret of the jars? Jason wondered. Tears prickled in his eyes, and he willed himself not to let them fall. *Chiron will live. He has to live.*

Jason spent a fitful night, starting awake every time Chiron twitched or groaned. Near morning, when the old centaur seemed the worst, breathing out in long, rattling rales, Jason went to the door of the cave and got down on his knees. He'd never prayed to the Fates before, though Chiron had taught him many prayers, yet this prayer seemed simply to breathe from his lips.

"O Moirai, allotters of life, of death, hear me.
Clotho holding the distaff, hear me,
Lachesis drawing the thread, hear me,
Atropos with the abhorred shears, hear me,

Do not cut short this good creature's time.
He is a teacher whose students need him.
He is a healer whose patients need him."

Here Jason took a deep breath, then ended:

"He is a father whose only son needs him."

This time the tears fell unchecked from his eyes and left streaks along his cheeks. He didn't bother to brush them away.

"Jason . . ." It was scarcely a whisper. It sounded more like a feeble breath of air hissing through a crack in a wall.

Jason scrambled back to Chiron on his hands and knees and put his ear close to the old centaur's mouth.

"Jason . . ."

"I'm here, Chiron, I'm here."

"The jars . . ." Chiron croaked. He made a movement as if trying to get up.

Jason put a hand on his shoulder to hold him down. "They're gone."

Chiron's eyelids drooped wearily, and he nodded. "Of course, you thought to look. You remembered after all this time."

"The door is open," Jason said. "Nessus didn't even bother to close it back up."

"He knew I had the jars," Chiron wheezed. "Demanded

I give them to him. I refused. Tried to stop them but could not. Now the power is his."

"What power? What's in those jars?"

"Gorgon's blood."

Jason sat back on his heels. "I don't understand. What would the centaurs want with Gorgon's blood?"

"The power of life and death."

Jason shook his head. "I still don't . . ."

"Surely you remember the story I told you."

Jason said softly, "Forgive me, master, you have told me many stories."

"Of the great hero Perseus."

"Ah," Jason said, nodding. "Perseus. How he hunted down Medusa, the most fearsome of the three Gorgons."

Chiron smiled and pushed up to a sitting position despite Jason's protests.

"Of course I remember," Jason said. "Her hair was made of snakes and her face was so ugly, the sight of it turned men to stone." He also remembered shivering in fear when Chiron first told him the story. He'd only been six years old then. "But what about the blood?"

"When Perseus cut off her head," Chiron said, "there were two veins in her severed neck. The blood that flowed from the left vein is the deadliest poison in all the world. The merest drop of it can kill a man instantly."

"And in the right vein?"

Chiron struggled to his feet. "The blood from there is

a medicine that can heal any wound or cure any sickness."

Jason caught his breath. It took a moment to digest all this. But then he asked, "How did the Gorgon's blood get here?"

Chiron gave himself a shake all over before replying. "Long before you ever came to Mount Pelion, another child was put in my care. Asclepius, the son of the god Apollo."

"You have said that name to me before, master."

Smiling, the old centaur went on. "I raised him, taught him as I have taught you. He had the most marvelous aptitude for medicine and healing. When he grew to manhood, the goddess Athena appeared and placed the two jars of Gorgon's blood in his care."

Jason shook his head. "But why doesn't he carry the jars with him? Why leave them here?"

"Ah, that is a sad tale," said Chiron. He stretched his arms and winced as pain shot through them. "But I best sit to tell it."

Jason helped him down again.

Once he was settled, the old centaur said, "That is better."

"Asclepius . . ." Jason prompted.

"Ah yes, Asclepius traveled far and wide," Chiron said, "tending the sick and bringing about many marvelous cures using the potions and herbal remedies I had taught him. But sometimes, if the need was great, he would use the healing blood of Medusa." He paused and looked at the roof of the cave, shuddering. Jason didn't know if Chiron was trembling with pain or with the memory.

"Then one day Asclepius went too far. He used the blood to raise a dead man back to life."

"Surely that's not possible!" Jason exclaimed. "Only the gods would dare to do such a thing."

"Which is what Zeus, the king of the gods, thought, too," said Chiron. "He struck Asclepius down with a thunderbolt. Before he died, however, Asclepius entrusted the jars to me. I made that secret hiding place, believing no one would ever find them there." Chiron stopped and coughed three times. Spasms shook his body, and he had to recover his breath before speaking again. "I would have died rather than surrender the Gorgon's blood, but Nessus already knew where it was hidden."

"Surely . . ." Jason framed his questions carefully. "Surely you don't think *I* told him anything!"

Chiron managed to summon a reassuring smile. "No, Jason, I know you have kept your vow."

"Then how . . ." But he'd already guessed. "When Nessus came to be healed."

"Yes, by the time he managed to get here, he was so badly wounded, none of my cures helped. Curse me, I could not face watching one of my own kind die a slow, painful death, even a wild, unruly centaur like Nessus. So

I used a drop of Gorgon's blood to heal him. I thought he was unconscious when I went to fetch the blue jar, the jar of healing. But I know now that he must have seen me and thus knew the hiding place. He must have remembered that I had taught Asclepius."

"Why does he want the jars? He's not a healer."

"Remember." Chiron's voice trembled as if he'd aged overnight. "The second jar, the red jar, is not for healing. Rather it brings death, swift and unstoppable."

Jason went cold all over. He knew before the old centaur spoke what he was going to say.

"I fear Nessus has always intended to commit some terrible wrong. And now he has the power to do it."

CHAPTER FIVE

A MATTER OF PRINCES

"Chiron, you're awake!"

The happy cry came from Melampus as he strode into the cave, a broad grin spread across his face. The other boys pressed close behind, looking just as pleased as he did.

"Stay back!" Melampus said, turning round and waving them off. "He needs room to breathe."

"Nothing like a beating to gather friends," Chiron muttered to Jason.

"It was those centaurs, wasn't it? Nessus and the others," Admetus asked.

"If our paths ever cross again . . ." said Idas, grinding his knuckles together.

"I am afraid your paths *will* cross again," Chiron said

weakly, waving a hand at the boys, "for you must follow the centaurs and retrieve what they stole from me."

"They stole something from you?" Idas blurted out.

"What did they steal?" asked Lynceus.

"Two clay jars."

"What's in them?" Acastus asked. "Gold? Jewels?"

"Nothing that would profit any of you directly," Chiron said, "but . . ." He hesitated, as if weighing his next words carefully. "But in the wrong hands, those jars hold great danger for all humankind."

The boys seemed to take a single deep breath and hold it.

"But danger especially," the old centaur added, "for the people of Iolcus."

Eyes narrowed, Acastus asked, "What do you mean?"

"I mean," Chiron said, "that something within the jars could be used by Nessus and his herd against their old enemies."

The boys waited to hear more, hardly moving, and Chiron said gruffly, "Will you, prince of Iolcus, stand by and do nothing?"

"If Iolcus is in danger, I will not be found wanting." Acastus' hand went to the medallion at his chest.

Chiron cleared his throat. "Then, Acastus, you must listen to Jason and follow Nessus and his herd. It will take a band of *heroes* to get those jars back here, where I will put them out of the way of the centaurs forever."

Acastus began to look interested. "You mean that the

poets will sing of us in years to come?"

"The songs, my young prince," said Chiron, "will be many and fine."

Face creased with worry, Admetus asked, "But how can we possibly catch up to them? They run as fast as horses, and we've no chariots to chase them with."

"Come," said Chiron. "Sit by me. I will explain all."

The boys all took up squatting positions in front of Chiron.

"Nessus and his troublemakers won't have traveled by night. They are day wanderers and will be easy to track, for they never think far enough ahead to try and disguise their passage."

The boys nodded at that, and Idas nudged Lynceus.

"Now they are probably resting and drinking, for they are easily distracted from their purpose," added Chiron.

"That's true," Idas said. "Yesterday, one minute they were ready to fight, the next they were on to something else. Jason warned us to wait them out, and he was right." There was grudging admiration in his voice.

Chiron nodded. "No discipline—that has always been their weakness. Otherwise they might well have been victorious over the men of Thessaly many years ago."

"Distracted or not, there are twelve of them at least," Admetus reminded his friends. "And who knows how many more are out there? How can six of us overcome them?"

"Certainly not by force of arms," said Chiron. "So you will have to use stealth—and your wits."

"Stealth and wits!" Acastus exclaimed. "What kind of heroes would we be then? What we want is an army. I could go to my father and—"

"No!" Chiron interrupted. The force of his cry drained him, and he slumped to the floor while the boys stood agape.

Quickly Jason knelt on one side, Melampus on the other. They supported Chiron as he sucked in a deep breath. "There is no time. You must set out after Nessus *now*." His eyes closed and his head bowed wearily as he whispered, "It is a matter of life and death."

Seeing that the boys were all looking dubiously at one another, Jason said with as much sarcasm as he could muster, "What happened to the idea of being heroes and having songs made to praise us?"

"A true warrior doesn't charge into battle without knowing what he's fighting for," said Admetus.

"You'll be fighting for Chiron," said Jason. "And for Iolcus. And for yourselves, too. Idas, don't you want a chance to pay the centaurs back for that tail-whipping across the face?"

For a moment Idas' eyes flashed angrily at the memory.

"And you, Acastus, remember that they called us women! Didn't you vow that you would meet them again with weapons?"

Now the boys all stared at Acastus, for it was clear there was only one answer a prince of Iolcus could give.

"We won't let our honor be unavenged," he declared. "We'll pay them back for their insults. And for what they've done to Chiron." It was well said, if a little late in the saying. Then he smiled. "And along the way we'll save all of Iolcus."

"Right," said Lynceus with a nervous grin, "the six of us will be more than a match for all of them."

"The *five* of us," said Jason. "Melampus needs to stay behind to take care of Chiron."

"Right, the five of us," said Lynceus, his grin falling apart. "*More* than enough." But his face spoke differently.

While Melampus changed Chiron's bandages and brewed a fresh herbal draught under the old centaur's directions, Jason and the others ate a quick breakfast. Then they began to collect their weapons and supplies.

The boys took a javelin and a short sword each. Admetus slung his bow on his back, while Lynceus stuffed a slingshot into his belt and hung a pouch of smooth stones there as well.

Jason's hand hovered between sling and bow, undecided. He was a better shot with the sling, having brought down many rabbits and partridge. And the bow would be an extra burden while scrambling up a mountain. But then he saw Acastus watching him, and he remembered how the Iolcus prince scorned the sling, calling it a peasant's weapon. "Fit only," he'd once said, "for those who have not the wealth to buy a bow nor the skill to make one."

Impulsively Jason snatched up the bow and a quiver of arrows, thinking, *Do you see, Acastus? I have chosen a prince's weapon.* But in his heart he felt a strange pang, as if he'd committed a betrayal.

While Idas and Admetus packed bundles of salted meat and fish, bread and cheese, Lynceus went to fill their water skins from the nearby spring.

"Better today than yesterday," Acastus said. "If we'd been this well armed then, none of those centaurs would have made it this far."

Idas nodded his agreement, but Admetus seemed not so certain. "Or we could all be dead on that hillside," he said.

Secretly Jason agreed. After all, they were just boys, not men. And while he knew himself good with the javelin, having killed wolves and deer before he was even twelve, he didn't know if he was strong enough to go up against centaurs. Chiron was right. They would have to use their wits and a good helping of stealth.

"What do you say, Jason?" Idas asked.

"I say we fight first, boast after."

Acastus laughed. "I think that Goat Boy is afraid."

Jason left them to finish the packing and went back to talk with Chiron. The centaur dismissed Melampus with thanks and beckoned Jason closer.

"I don't like to leave you this way," Jason said.

Chiron waved his concerns aside. "Though he is no Asclepius, young Melampus is already a skilled physician. He will take good care of me. Besides, I'm stronger than you think. It is difficult to kill off an old centaur."

"If we only had the Gorgon's blood—" Jason began.

Chiron cut him off. "Nature will heal me without any such aid. To use it without need is to insult the gods and anger the Fates. Promise me you will never even *think* of using the blood. And be sure you stop Nessus before he does."

Jason bit his lower lip. "Master, perhaps Acastus is right. Perhaps we do need to find help."

"I was not entirely honest with you, my boy," Chiron said. "It is not only the time that matters. Secrecy also matters. No one else must know what those jars hold. Think what would happen if the Gorgon's blood were to fall into the hands of King Pelias or any other tyrant. That would be as bad as letting Nessus have it."

"Is the king such a bad man?"

Chiron was silent for a moment, then said, "He has his son Acastus' worst qualities magnified a hundred times, and with no one to speak to him of justice and virtue."

Jason tried to imagine such a creature. It made him shiver.

"No," Chiron said, "Pelias must not even hear of the

Gorgon's blood. The fewer who know of its existence, the better. Do not tell the boys what is in those jars. Just that it is something with which humans must not tamper."

"But are we five strong enough to take on those wild centaurs?"

"I know you are only boys, Jason. Still, you all have spirit and courage. However, *you* will have to lead them, for only *you* have the wit for it, and the knowledge of the mountains. Only *you* can find the centaurs in time."

"How can *I* lead them? They are all nobly born, while I . . ." Jason hated the whine in his voice, but somehow he couldn't seem to control it.

Chiron rubbed his eyes and let out a deep sigh. "I knew this day would come, but I did not think it would be so soon."

"Knew what day would come?" Jason leaned toward him.

Regarding him squarely, Chiron said, "You have every right to be their leader, Jason, for you are no lost orphan, though I have always let you think so."

Jason gaped at the centaur. "Then who am I?"

"You are the rightful prince of Iolcus."

Jason laughed out loud. "And my father, I suppose, is the king of the gods, mighty Zeus. Nessus must have landed an awful blow to your head, master. You're raving."

Chiron did not look away but stared steadily at Jason.

"But Acastus' father, Pelias, is king of Iolcus," Jason said.

"In name only," said Chiron. "In truth it is your father, Aeson, who should be sitting upon the throne."

"My *father* . . ." The word suddenly sounded so strange. All these years he'd been told his parents were dead. *No,* he thought, *this is too fantastic.* He shook his head. "You're only saying these things because you want me to find the Gorgon's blood. It's another one of your stories."

"It is the truth," said Chiron. "A truth I was sworn to keep from you till the time was right. Sit close and listen, and I will tell it to you quickly, for you must not delay much longer."

Jason refused to sit, watching as the old centaur shifted, trying to find a position in which his injuries did not hurt him too much. "When Cretheus, your grandfather, was king of Iolcus, he took a foreign wife named Tyro. She gave him three sons: your father, Aeson; Pheres, who is the father of Admetus; and a third son, Amphythaon, who sired Melampus."

"I am cousin to Admetus and Melampus?" Jason was too stunned to ask more.

Chiron nodded.

Then Jason blurted out, "So who is Pelias?"

"Tyro's son from an earlier marriage, a brute and a bully even as a child, who was much indulged by his mother, for he was the only one like her in looks and temper. Your grandfather was a kind man who cared for young Pelias as though he were a true son. Alas that it should have been so. The gods have a strange sense of humor sometimes."

"I think I would have liked my grandfather," said Jason, his disbelief fast fading.

"By the time old Cretheus died, Pelias had gathered a band of strong-armed warriors around him and took control of the palace, claiming it his as the eldest son, even though he was no blood of the king."

"But," Jason objected, "then he had no right to the throne."

"No, but once a cruel and ruthless man has seized power, it takes a stronger man than your father to unseat him," said Chiron. "And Aeson had always been a kind and simple soul who had no thirst for power or glory. Nor did he want to plunge his beloved Iolcus into a bloody civil war. In fact, his clear lack of ambition was all that kept him alive with that bullying older half brother in power. He was simply no threat at all. He retreated to a country house with his scrolls and his music and lived a quiet life. There he married in secret, a woman as kind and retiring as he. But when she gave birth to a son, Aeson feared that Pelias would see the child as a threat to his own heir, Acastus. So Aeson did the bravest thing he'd ever done in his life—he kept your very existence a secret and brought you to me to be raised and protected, to be prepared for the day you would return to Iolcus to reclaim your birthright."

It was a thrilling story, but all it did was make Jason angry. "Why didn't you tell me before? All these years I thought . . . I thought I was no one."

"If you believe that, then I have failed you indeed," said Chiron sadly. "But hear my reasons: I could say nothing, for I had sworn an oath to keep your identity secret. And to me such an oath is a sacred pledge. For think about it—if Pelias were to find out who you are, he would have you killed without a moment's hesitation. After all, his half brother Aeson is already long discredited by his own reticence. But a son, young, strong, heroic—with a genuine claim to the throne—ah, that would be seen as a real threat!"

The old centaur waited a moment, gazing long into his young student's drawn face. "Do you believe me, Jason?"

Jason turned and, with his back to Chiron, said, "I no longer know what to believe."

In the shadow of the cave entrance Acastus pressed a fist to his mouth to keep from uttering a curse. He'd crept in stealthily, hoping to overhear some clue as to what was contained in the mysterious jars. But what he'd learned was far different.

So, he mused, *Jason is the son of that feeble graybeard Aeson whom Father despises so much.* As he slipped back out into the morning sunshine before Jason left the old centaur's side, Acastus' mind roiled with bad thoughts.

"What right does that old fool have to the crown of Iolcus?" he whispered to himself. "What right does Jason have?" He stopped and looked around the clearing where the others were finishing up the packing. "It takes a strong man to rule. A man like Father," he muttered. "A man like me."

Looking back at the cave with hatred in his eyes, Acastus thought, *With enough supporters Jason could indeed pose a real threat to our rule.* He was not unaware of Jason's skills, much as he disliked him. The wily old Chiron had taught Jason well. Whatever the outcome of this mission, Acastus was certain of one thing: *Jason must not return from it alive.*

CHAPTER SIX

THE TUG OF A ROPE

Before setting out on their mission, the boys lined up to make their farewells to Chiron.

"You must follow Jason's lead," said Chiron, his voice thin and reedy. He had propped himself up unsteadily on one elbow, and there were dark shadows under his eyes. "Jason knows the countryside, and I have been instructing him for many years."

"Instructing him in what?" Acastus drawled. "How to plant onions and tend sheep?" He was leaning against the wall with a smirk on his face that suggested he knew something no one else did.

The other boys shot quick glances at one another, clearly taken aback by his arrogance at a time like this.

A shadow of pain flitted across Chiron's face, and

Jason decided to spare the old centaur further effort by answering for him. "How to track and forage. How to stay out of sight. And how to fight. Is that enough, Acastus?"

Acastus looked away. "I was just asking," he answered in a bored voice.

Raising his hand, Admetus said, "Do we even know in which direction to start?"

Melampus cleared his throat and stepped forward. "I can answer that. According to the birds, the centaurs headed toward the northwest. If you go that way you should pick up their trail."

"I'll keep a lookout for their tracks," said Lynceus.

Chiron nodded. "Good, you are already thinking like a team. With Jason at your head, you will all go far." He paused for a moment and drew in a deep breath. "If, as you say, Melampus, the centaurs are heading northwest, they are most likely going to Mount Ossa. That is the traditional gathering place of our people in time of war."

"War?" Idas gulped. "Is there going to be a war?"

Suddenly alert, Acastus leaned forward. "It's because of those jars, isn't it?"

Chiron quickly changed the subject. "If they're going toward Mount Ossa, they'll have to turn west, toward the lower country."

Admetus understood first. "They can gallop faster across open ground."

Chiron nodded at him.

"And a lot faster than we can go," Idas noted grimly.

"That's why we aren't going to follow them," said Jason.

All eyes turned toward him. He had been giving this business a lot of thought, and now it was time to tell them what he had in mind.

"We'll go directly north," he said.

"You mean straight across the mountains?" said Acastus. His mouth twisted. "It would be easier to fly like one of Melampus' birds."

"Yes. It will be hard," Jason admitted, "but it can be done. I've spoken to hunters who have made the ascent. We can pick up the centaurs' trail on the other side. Or are you not up to the challenge?"

In answer, Acastus turned his back to Jason and stared out at a high tree.

"Around the mountains or over them," said Idas, "it makes no difference to me. I've business to settle."

"And I." Admetus put his fist to his chest.

"And I," Lynceus added.

Only Acastus was silent.

Jason looked to Chiron, who nodded proudly. "It is your best chance," the centaur said. "But only if you keep your purpose before you and trust in one another. For that is what the virtuous man does: puts the purpose ahead of his personal discomforts and concerns. Always stay together. When one falls, another must lift him up. Only in this way can you succeed."

The boys exchanged uneasy glances, as if having to cooperate were more of an obstacle than the mountains.

"We will succeed, Chiron," Jason promised, wishing he were even half as confident as he was trying to sound.

Suddenly Chiron groaned wearily. Melampus rushed to his side to wipe his brow with a damp linen cloth. Gradually he coaxed the centaur into lying down again.

"You should go now," he said to his friends, "so that you waste no more time. And—so Chiron can rest."

Weapons in hand, and supplies in packs tied onto their backs, the boys set off down the slope toward the great spur of rock that connected Mount Pelion to the cluster of mountains to the north. Beyond them lay the valley of Hecla and the mountain of Ossa.

Each of them cast a final backward glance at the humble caves that had been their home these past months. Though they had set out before on hunting and foraging expeditions, this time was different. This time they did not know if they would ever return.

A weird silence hung over the little band as Jason led them around the northern slopes. There was none of the usual bantering, the joke telling, the occasional bursts of song. It was as if there were something everyone wanted to talk about but no one dared mention.

On one particularly tricky bit of ridge, Jason led the way and the others fanned out single file behind him. When he got to the end of that ridge, he went on ahead, stopping at last, breathing hard. He pointed to a longer, rockier ridge that was the next step on their route. "That's going to be even more treacherous. Are you ready for it?"

There was no response, and he looked around. The others had stopped some distance behind him. He walked back and noticed that they could not meet his eyes.

"What's the matter?" Jason asked. "Have you all gone lame?"

Idas drew himself up to his full height—which was at least a head taller than Jason's. "Before we go farther we need to settle who is to be the leader of this band."

Jason's fingers clenched tightly around his javelin. "You all heard what Chiron said. He wants you to follow me."

Glancing back along the ridge they had just traversed, Idas said, "Chiron is a long way off now. He may not even be alive when we get back. The choice should be ours, not his."

"Besides," Admetus added, "why should you be in charge? Acastus and I are princes." He paused and gazed sidelong at Acastus, waiting for him to say something. But the prince of Iolcus was oddly silent, as if content to let Admetus make the argument.

"We're not in a palace now," said Jason, "and we've no army to lead. It doesn't matter who your father is out here."

"Or who he isn't?" Acastus suddenly put in.

Idas was thinking. His furrowed brow announced as much. At last he said, "Strength matters more than birth here on these mountains. And later, when we fight the centaurs, it will matter even more. Now no one would disagree that I am the strongest. So—who better to take charge than I?"

"Idas is right in his own way," said Lynceus, who had been silent till that moment. "But of course some might think the person leading should have remarkably keen eyesight, so that he could spot any danger lying ahead."

Idas cuffed him across the ear.

"Ow!" Lynceus cried.

"You didn't see that danger coming, did you, brother?" Idas guffawed.

"No, but I can see what's crawling up your leg."

As soon as Idas looked down, Lynceus started to laugh. "At least I don't look where there's nothing to see!"

Idas took another swipe at him, but Lynceus ducked under the blow and backed away.

"There's no point in you two arguing," Admetus said. "Leadership is a matter of royal blood. Everyone knows that. So the choice of leader is between Acastus and me."

"Maybe we *should* let you lead the way," drawled Acastus. "Then, when you fall headlong down the first crevasse we come to, I can take over."

Admetus' face flushed. "You think so much of yourself, Acastus, but everybody knows it's a stolen throne you stand to inherit!"

Acastus lofted his spear into a throwing position. "If you speak to me like that again," he warned through gritted teeth, "I'll send you back to that dung heap you call a kingdom with a spear in your belly."

"Stop it!" At the sound of Jason's voice, they all went still and Acastus lowered his weapon. "You are acting like boys playing at tug the rope. All of you want to give orders and none of you wants to take them."

"And are you any different?" Acastus drawled.

"Chiron obviously thought so," Jason said quietly, but the others laughed.

Idas thumped his spear butt on the ground. "We need to settle this fairly, by a contest of skill and strength."

"And who's going to decide the rules for that?" Lynceus asked suspiciously.

"We don't have time for this," Jason pleaded. "Let's just move forward and decide all this afterward."

"I don't think you have much support, Goat Boy," said Acastus, his voice dripping with sarcasm.

Thinking desperately, Jason tried to recall what he and Chiron had discussed about leadership, about the qualities of kings and warlords. At the time he hadn't understood why he should have to learn about such things. Now he knew.

"Any man can shout orders and enforce his will by fear," Chiron had said. "A true leader is one others follow because they choose to."

"But what if they don't choose to follow?" Jason remembered asking.

Chiron had grinned. "There's always a way to persuade them. Everyone has a weak spot, some matter of vanity that can be used to tug him forward, like a rope around the neck of a stubborn mule."

Slowly Jason looked around at each of the boys in turn. He could think of nothing to say that would persuade all of them as a group, but over the past weeks he had come to know each of them well, better perhaps than they suspected. *If not all at once*, he told himself, *perhaps one at a time.*

"Lynceus," he said, taking a step closer to Idas' sharp-eyed brother, "once we're over the mountains, we'll need you to spy out the centaurs' trail. You can do that for us, can't you?"

Lynceus nodded uncertainly, not sure where this was leading.

Jason turned to the two princes. "Once we've found the centaurs," he said, "we'll need someone trained in strategy to come up with a plan to overcome them. We'll be depending on you, Acastus and Admetus, to do that, or all will be lost."

Bristling, Admetus asked, "Do you think we can't?"

"I'm sure you can," Jason answered confidently.

Acastus narrowed his eyes and gave the slightest of nods.

Idas flexed his broad shoulders. "What about me?" he

demanded, a menacing gleam in his eye.

"If it comes to a fight, Idas," Jason said, "there's no one any of us would rather have in the forefront of the battle than you. And I'm certain that's where you want to be."

Idas appeared satisfied with this and relaxed his threatening posture.

"But none of that will count for anything unless we reach Mount Ossa in time to learn the centaurs' plans," Jason went on. He placed a hand on his chest. "That's my task, to get us all safely over the mountains. Does anybody think he can do that better than I can?"

"Jason does know the route better than any of us," Idas conceded, rubbing his square jaw.

"So really you'll be a sort of guide," said Admetus.

"I don't care what you choose to call me, but we have to go on—now!" Jason said.

There was a long pause as the boys all mulled this over. Then Acastus broke the silence.

"You go ahead, Jason," he said. "I'll be happy to watch your back."

Something in the prince's tone sent shivers along Jason's spine, but to his relief he saw the others nodding their agreement. Seizing the opportunity, he turned and started off across the slope. He was glad they couldn't see the sweat pouring down his brow as if he'd just stuck his head in a stream.

CHAPTER SEVEN

THE NARROW PATH

idday they reached the steep, barren ridge that stretched from the northern slopes of Pelion to the main mass of mountains. The ridge was like a long curtain of gray and yellow rock stretching down to the wooded, boulder-strewn valley below.

"There's a path here," Jason said, pointing. "A narrow ledge, but passable."

Lynceus squinted along the line of Jason's finger. "There's a path all right," he agreed. "But it's hardly wide enough for a goat."

"If it's good enough for a goat, it's good enough for you," said Idas.

"Then what are we waiting for?" Admetus asked.

The start of the path was a narrow ribbon of stone

clinging to the rock face. Below was a drop of at least a hundred feet to treetops that were like a row of spear points waiting to impale anyone who fell.

"Who's going to go first?" asked Admetus.

"Jason, of course." Acastus smiled slowly. "He's our guide, after all."

Jason ignored the sting in Acastus' words and nodded. "Keep close together, but leave enough space that you aren't jostling one another." He set out boldly, wanting to show confidence, though there was a hollow in the pit of his stomach.

Acastus shouldered Admetus aside and followed immediately behind him. When Jason glanced back, Acastus grinned. "I told you I'd watch your back, Jason."

Not to be outdone, Admetus went next, his face a scowl.

"I'll go last," said Idas, shoving his brother on ahead of him.

Lynceus staggered forward under the force of the push. "Why should I go next?" he asked resentfully.

"Because if you were last, brother, you might just think better of it and turn back."

"Well, if any goats come along after us," Lynceus joked, "you're the one who'll have to fight them off."

At first the path was a good three feet wide, wide enough for even Idas to walk comfortably. However, the surface was bumpy and strewn with jagged fragments of flint that pressed hard into the soles of their sandals.

Before they were halfway across, the footing started to shrink inches at a time.

Jason halted and raised a warning hand. Turning his head, he called out, "It gets narrower here. You're all going to have to space out a bit more."

He heard grunting agreement behind him, and he started forward again, but carefully.

Soon the only way they could continue was to turn with their noses scraping against the rough wall. Encumbered as they were with weapons and supplies, they couldn't set their backs to the mountain, and they were all mindful of the drop behind them.

Lynceus said loudly, "It's going to be hard for Idas to go much farther, big as he is."

"Don't you worry about me," Idas rumbled. "You just mind your own footing."

"It's all right," Admetus said, struggling to sound confident. "Jason's been this way before, so it must be safe."

Jason reached out with a toe and kicked a troublesome rock off the path ahead. "I never said I'd been this way before."

There was a stunned silence as the other boys paused in midstep. The sound of the rock tumbling down the drop, hitting against occasional outcroppings, was ominous.

"You told us you knew the route," Acastus said in a low, accusing voice. "You said there was a way over the mountains."

Jason took a deep breath, then let it out slowly. "I've

spoken to hunters who've crossed here."

"Hunters!" squeaked Lynceus. "Those braggarts will say anything for a cup of wine!"

"They were telling the truth," Jason insisted. "The path is here, isn't it?"

"So far." Admetus groaned.

"So," Acastus said, voice dripping venom, "all you know of the route over the mountains is what you've heard from others?"

Jason knew he could not afford to show weakness when all of them were so uncertain and in such a vulnerable position on the mountain ridge.

"That's right," he replied. "Why? Do you want to run away? If you do, you'll have to persuade the others to go first."

There was another long silence as they contemplated inching back the way they'd come.

At last, in a quavering voice, Admetus asked, "Is there anything else you haven't told us?"

"Oh, I'm sure there are a lot of things Jason hasn't told us," Acastus said darkly. "And sooner or later, one of them is going to trip him up. We have to hope they don't trip us up as well."

Heart pounding, his chest pressed against the rock, Jason bit down hard on his lower lip. Had he really let them think he knew the way better than he did? He was sure he hadn't planned to deceive them. On the other hand, if they had known the truth, would they have come even this far? Then he remembered why he'd brought them this way. The goal was more important than any of their complaints.

"Enough talk," barked Idas. "My legs are getting stiff standing here. Let's move along. If we fall to our deaths, we can beat Jason into a paste when we catch up with him in the Underworld."

Lynceus laughed weakly. "Yes, that will be something to look forward to."

"It *would* be as hard to go back now as it would be to continue," Admetus added.

Jason devoutly hoped that was true, and resumed his sideways movement along the ledge. But he was more worried than he let on. If the ridge grew any narrower he doubted they could make it. Certainly not with their heavy packs. Even now, he thought, it would only take a gust of wind to blow them off. Or the slip of a foot.

Beside him, the boys were still quarreling.

"Admetus, you fool, leave me some room!" Acastus hissed.

"The end of your spear is poking my leg."

And then the very thing that Jason had feared happened. Acastus' flash of temper caused his concentration to lapse. Some loose stones slid out from under the prince's foot and went rattling down the dizzy slope, throwing him off balance. For a second he struggled to right himself, clawing at the rough wall with his free hand, trying to find a grip.

Jason reached out and clasped him by the shoulder to steady him. Instead of being grateful for the help, the prince flattened himself against the rock face and slapped Jason's arm away impatiently.

"I don't need your assistance!" he snapped.

Jason felt a spark of anger but quickly quenched it. This was far too dangerous a spot for a fight. "Next time I won't bother," he muttered, working his way farther along the ledge.

Two sliding steps more and Jason found he suddenly had room to move. Looking ahead, he saw that the path was definitely broadening out again. He beamed.

"It gets easier from here," he called to the others.

He had hardly begun to enjoy his sense of relief when a startled cry made him look back. Lynceus had lost his balance and was toppling backward. His arms were spinning frantically. His javelin had gone flying from his hand and was hurtling end over end through the air.

In the blink of an eye, Idas had tossed his own spear away and dug his fingers into a cleft in the rock, scraping the flesh from them. With his other hand he snatched hold of Lynceus' belt just as his brother's feet slipped off the edge.

For an instant Lynceus dangled in space, his eyes bulging in panic. Only the strength of his brother's arm was keeping him from his doom. Then Idas swung Lynceus back, slamming him into the rock so hard, his face was almost flattened.

"You . . . can . . . let . . . go . . . now." Lynceus gasped, his lips rasping against the stone wall.

Idas released his grip and flexed his arm with a scowl. "I've thrown away my best spear to save you," he grumbled. "I'm not sure it was a good trade."

The other boys laughed nervously before moving on.

It took another half hour to reach the end of the ridge. By that time every muscle in Jason's body was aching and his legs felt as though they had turned into stalks of straw. He thought, *If I feel this way, I can only imagine how the others are doing.* But he kept those thoughts to himself. As leader—or guide—he had to be strong.

Scrambling up onto the mountain slope like a half-drowned man dragging himself onto the shore, he checked to see where they were. The area was dotted with pricker bushes and shriveled trees that had to survive on what little rainwater seeped into the cracks in the hard rock, but it was the sweetest piece of land Jason had ever set eyes on.

He flung himself down flat on the ground and breathed easily for what seemed the first time in hours.

One by one the others flopped down beside him, panting and groaning.

Lynceus let out a squeaky laugh. "If I knew which god to thank for getting me across safely, I'd build him a temple right here."

"You've me to thank," said Idas, "and I don't want a temple."

"Good," Lynceus gasped. "I haven't the strength for building one anyway."

"I say we eat something and then move on," Jason said.

"Move on?" Admetus and Lynceus spoke as one, and Idas shook his head. Only Acastus, sitting apart from the others, refused comment.

"Move on," Jason repeated, "because this is no place to spend the night." He gestured to the hard, open ground and the gray, dying trees.

After a brief meal the boys resumed their trek, but silently, as if adding words to their burdens would have been more weight than they could carry.

Working their way around the curve of the slope involved clambering over boulders, squeezing through tight gaps, and then clawing their way up steep inclines littered with loose pebbles. But after the trial they had just completed, no one complained.

Once they were on a safer path, Jason let his mind wander back to his last conversation with Chiron. He gnawed on it like a wolf on a bone. How *could* the old centaur have let him spend all these years thinking he was a nobody, a goat boy, with no family and no home? Wouldn't his life have been different if he'd known from the start that his grandfather had been a king? That his father was alive and had sent him away for safety? That in his own right he should be king?

Then he shook his head. What had being raised as a prince done for Acastus? Only made him selfish and arrogant and unwilling to learn. Of course Admetus was a prince, too, and not so unpleasant. But look at all the time he wasted trying to prove to Acastus he was just as important.

Perhaps, Jason thought, *it hasn't been so bad growing up in a mountain cave, far from the centers of power and riches. If only*—he could not get the thought out of his head—*if only I'd known.*

The sun was sinking as they descended the far slope, and at first they did not see what lay ahead. It was Lynceus who let out a cry, alerting the others.

Cutting directly across their path was a vast chasm. It stretched off into the distance to both right and left. As far as any of them could see, there was no possible way across.

"What now, Goat Boy?" asked Acastus.

Jason wished he had an answer.

CHAPTER EIGHT

THE CHASM

They moved down in silence toward the edge of the chasm. Far below, almost lost in the shadows, a ribbon of water gurgled and foamed around jagged rocks that jutted up like fangs.

Helplessly they gazed both east and west.

"I suppose your hunter friends just flapped their arms and flew across this?" Acastus' sarcasm was like the crack of a whip.

"They *did* get across," Jason answered feebly, desperately racking his brain to remember what they had said.

"I knew we were fools to trust him," Admetus muttered.

"Not so long ago you were playing the lamb to his shepherd," Acastus said. "If he walked over the edge of this hole, you'd probably follow him to your doom."

"Sooner that than follow you, Acastus!" Admetus exclaimed.

The two princes clenched their fists and glared at each other.

"I've a good mind to knock your heads together," said Idas.

"Oh, let them fight it out, Idas," said his brother.

"There *is* a way," Jason declared, stepping between them. "I remember it now. It's farther west, a spot where the gap narrows to only a few feet. It can be jumped there."

"Really?" Acastus raised a skeptical eyebrow. "Is that the best you can do? Can't you just admit you were wrong?"

Lynceus stared hard toward the west. Suddenly he pointed. "There." His finger held true. "There is a place where our side juts out into the gap."

"Then let's take a look," said Idas, slapping his brother on the back.

They practically sprinted westward along the side of the chasm, but when they reached the place that Lynceus had spotted, Jason's heart sank. Even on the very edge of this promontory, the gap between their side and the other was twenty feet across at least.

"There must be *another* place," Jason said without much hope in his voice. He put a hand up to shade his eyes and looked around, but the ravine seemed bigger and the gap across wider the longer he stared at it.

Meanwhile Lynceus was checking the way they had come, then ahead, but finally he said dismally, "Nothing within half a day's trek of here. And that would take us back round to the south. Not exactly where we want to go."

"I suppose we could just retreat," said Admetus. "Try to find another way around."

"And lose two or three days in the process." Acastus looked grim. "By the time we reached Mount Ossa, the centaurs would be long gone, and those cursed jars of Chiron's with them."

While they argued, Lynceus sank down on his hands and knees, examining the ground.

"Look here," he said suddenly, "at the edge of the stone." They gathered around him but didn't know what they were supposed to be seeing, so Lynceus explained. "There's no moss growing on it, and it's hardly been touched by the weather."

"So?"

"That means it's fresh stone. A chunk of rock must have broken off from here, and recently, too."

"There was that earthquake a few months ago," Admetus recalled, "before we all came up Mount Pelion to study with Chiron."

"Yes," Acastus said. "I remember. My father ordered a dozen bulls sacrificed to appease Poseidon, earth shatterer."

"The earthquake must have caused the rock to break," said Jason. "So up until then this *was* the way across."

"Well, that *explains* it," said Idas, "but it doesn't help us. We're still stuck here on this side."

The boys all agreed, nodding.

"We followed your lead, Jason." Acastus gestured toward the yawning chasm. "And see what it's brought us to."

"That's not really Jason's fault," Admetus put in quickly.

"When you are leader, *everything* is your fault," said Acastus. "My father taught me that."

"And what would you have done differently?" Jason demanded. "Would this be any less of a dead end if you had been in charge? Did your father teach you to *fly*?"

"No, and he didn't teach me to hide either," Acastus retorted.

Hide? Jason wondered what Acastus meant. But before he could consider it further, Lynceus' voice caught his attention.

"It's only about twenty feet. That's not so far, is it?"

"Then you think you can jump it, brother?"

"Of course not." Lynceus made a face at Idas. "But perhaps we could build a bridge."

"Do you know how long it would take to build a bridge long enough to span that gap and strong enough not to collapse?" asked Acastus.

"We could cut down a tree and shove it across," said Idas, looking up at some of the trees that lined the slopes above them. None of them looked particularly sturdy.

"Even if we could find one tall enough, its own weight would topple it into the chasm before we could push it all the way over," said Lynceus.

This thought sobered them all, and they took off their packs and sat down near the edge. For a long moment they were silent, each considering the gulf before them.

At last Jason broke the silence. "Maybe we can make a bridge of sorts."

As one, they stared at him.

"Get a rope across, and fasten it at both ends," he explained. "We wrap our arms and legs around it and slide across one at a time."

"What? Hang over that drop?" Lynceus gulped. "You might as well just jump in and get it over with."

But Idas looked interested. Finger to his lip, he said, "It would have to be fixed securely."

Jason pointed. "Do you see those rocks on the far side?" He stood and Lynceus got up with him. Jason put a hand on Lynceus' shoulder. "Can you see a place where we might secure a hook of some sort?"

Lynceus stared hard for a few moments. "Yes," he said hesitantly. "But there's no guarantee the rope would hold."

"And we don't have a hook," Acastus pointed out. "Or did you think to hide one away in your tunic before we left?" He, too, stood and came over to stare across the chasm at the rocks.

Idas and Admetus scrambled to their feet, and soon all five of them were standing in a line on the chasm's edge.

"We can lash two swords together in a cross," said Jason. "We'll tie the rope to the center of the cross and throw it over. With any luck it should catch between the rocks. You can throw it that far, can't you, Idas?"

"Of course I can," said Idas. "Lynceus can point out the target to me."

"If it works, we won't have lost any time," said Jason. "And if it doesn't . . ." He shrugged. "Well, we won't be any worse off than before."

"Except for the swords," Acastus pointed out.

Taking his own sword and Admetus', Jason lashed them together with his belt so that they formed a cross of bronze.

Meanwhile, Idas unslung the rope from his shoulder and began unwinding it.

"It's barely long enough, Jason," he said grimly.

"That's all it needs to be," Jason said. He worked the end of the rope through the leather lashing and tied a double knot to hold it secure.

"You see," Lynceus pointed out to his brother, "there's a pair of rocks there, one sticking up like a finger, the other shaped like a shepherd's cap. Try and get the cross between them."

Idas said nothing, but his lips were pressed so hard together, they looked like one lip. With his right hand he gripped the end of the rope just below the makeshift grapple. Then, swinging his arm back and forth—once, twice—he threw the line across the gap on the third swing.

The crossed swords struck the ground just short of the target and slipped off the edge. Idas reeled them in, grinding his teeth in frustration. No one said a word as he started to swing the line again.

With a grunt he tossed it into the air, the bronze blades glinting in the sun. This time the metal cross struck the tall rock and bounced back into the chasm.

Idas let out an angry snarl, and no one ventured a word as he pulled the rope back up. Stepping as close as he dared to the edge of the chasm, Idas started swinging the line again. Under his breath he said what might have been a prayer—or a curse.

Up flew the swords, down they came—just beyond the two rocks.

"That's it!" Lynceus cried.

Idas beamed as he gave a tug and the swords locked in place.

"Does it look secure?" Jason asked.

Lynceus peered across the gap and shrugged. "They're fitted kind of awkwardly. I wouldn't like to trust myself to that."

"It's firm enough," said Idas, yanking on the rope.

"Pull harder," Acastus ordered.

"If it breaks free, then it's all been for nothing," Idas said.

"If it breaks when one of us is on it, it'll make *him* nothing," Acastus muttered.

Idas pulled. The swords seemed secure.

"You should let us help you hold the line," said Lynceus, reaching for the rope.

"I can manage it myself," said Idas, shrugging him away. "There's little enough of it to grip as is."

"But how will the last one get across?" Admetus wondered.

"I'll tie the line there," said Idas. He tilted his head in the direction of a sapling that was rooted in the ground about five feet from the cliff's edge.

"Are you sure it can take your weight?" Lynceus asked, giving the sapling a dubious stare.

"Are we going to stand around talking or are we going to get started?" Acastus demanded sharply.

"We'd better do it quickly, then," said Admetus. "We've no more than an hour of daylight left."

"Acastus is right," said Jason, stepping forward. "I'll go first."

Acastus stepped in front of Jason, blocking his way. "Why should you go first?"

"Because I led us here. Because being here, at an impossible chasm, is my fault and therefore my responsibility. Isn't that what your father would say?"

Acastus opened and closed his mouth like a fish, as if he could think of nothing to say in answer.

Jason wished he could take more satisfaction from that small victory, but the real challenge lay ahead. He walked around the prince and took a firm grip on the rope with both hands. Then he swung his feet up and crossed his ankles over the line.

Now he was hanging like a boar slung on a pole after a hunt. The sun had sunk so low, when he looked down he saw only darkness, which—he thought—was small comfort. He could hear water hissing unseen around the rocks below. The sound seemed to whisper to him, call to him. For an instant he felt as though the shadows were reaching up to pull him down. He turned his eyes away and fixed them on the far side of the chasm.

Seeing him waver, Admetus cried out, "Are you all right, Jason?"

Jason nodded and started to slide slowly along the rope, moving wormlike, a little bit at a time. The rope scraped his calves and before long all his muscles ached.

This was a stupid idea, he thought. *Acastus is right. What kind of a leader am I? And if I can't get across, how can the others?* His arms began to tremble and he worried about holding on.

Behind him, the other boys held their breath as they watched him inch along. Idas gripped the rope so tightly, the veins were standing out on the back of his broad hands.

Jason was all too aware of the fact that only a pair of short swords lashed with leather was holding him aloft. One wrong move might break his grip and send him plunging to his doom.

Oh, Poseidon, earth shatterer, he prayed, *hold the blades together.*

He wondered if the twelve bulls Acastus' father had given the god were enough. The gods could be incredibly greedy.

Suddenly he heard the makeshift grapple slip in its rock moorings, felt a horrible slackening of the line. Clenching his teeth against a scream, he sent up a silent cry for help: *O ye gods, don't let me fall.*

CHAPTER NINE

ONWARD AND UPWARD

Jason felt a cold sweat break out over every inch of his body, but the line held. There had been no cry of alarm from the other boys. Perhaps nothing had happened at all.

It's only my imagination, he told himself. What was it Chiron had said? He tried to remember. And then he had it: *There is no wound, no sickness, worse than the fear that grows in a man's own heart, for that is an enemy that attacks from within.*

But the worm in his mind said otherwise. If he was wrong, if the grapple was coming loose, his next move might pull it away altogether.

Suddenly he couldn't move.

"What's wrong?" he heard Lynceus mutter. "He looks

like he's turned to stone."

Jason twisted slightly, looked back, and saw Acastus place a hand on Idas' arm.

"Keep a tight hold," the prince was saying. "The slightest slackening of your grip could shake Jason loose."

Idas shrugged him off roughly. "Stand clear! This is hard enough without you getting in the way."

Acastus stepped away, but his eyes were still fixed on Jason.

Jason sucked in a deep breath. *I . . . won't . . . surrender . . . to . . . fear.* Gritting his teeth, he forced his muscles to move, his hands to slide forward a few inches. He worked his legs down after them.

The rope held.

Pressing on steadily, Jason went inch by painful inch until he felt his fingers touch the far side and scrape onto solid ground, and he dragged himself the rest of the way onto the land.

He heard a ragged cheer from his companions and lay on the ground with a foolish grin on his face, his exhaustion forgotten in the glow of triumph.

After his heart had stopped thudding, he got up and went over to examine the two swords. They *had* shifted, but downward, to a more stable position. So it hadn't been his imagination after all.

Pushing the grapple down even more securely, he took a grip on the rope. "Come on!" he called to the others. "We don't have all day!"

Admetus had been pushed into third place back at the ledge, but now he was quick to seize hold of the rope before Acastus could edge past him, almost as if he needed to take his turn while his courage still served him. Hooking his legs onto the line, he started shuffling out over the chasm. But his first rush of boldness soon deserted him, and he slowed down not even halfway across.

Jason saw Admetus' head hanging to one side, could see him shuddering, his arms and legs wrapped about the rope, like a baby clinging to its mother.

"What's the matter, Admetus?" Acastus called. "Did you forget something? Maybe you'd best come back for it." He was about to say something more, but Lynceus punched him hard on the arm.

"Shut up. Shut up." Lynceus' voice was low, his anger scarcely contained. "What if we did that to you?"

Admetus didn't move.

"Come on, Admetus," Jason called out, as calmly as he could. "You're most of the way here." Though in fact Admetus wasn't even a third of the way across.

"It's too far down," Admetus cried in a hoarse whisper. "I don't want to die, Jason."

"No, you don't," Jason agreed evenly. "That's why you've got to move before you get too tired to hang on."

"If I try to move I might fall." Admetus moaned. It sounded like the wind through a chasm.

"You're only in danger if you don't move," said Jason. "Don't look down. Close your eyes and listen to me."

Admetus closed his eyes. It seemed to cost him a lot of effort.

"Now come toward my voice. Just follow the thread of it," Jason said. "One hand. That's it. Now the other. Good. Good."

Admetus inched forward.

"Keep coming. See. I'm pulling you along. It's not just you on the rope. It's both of us. One hand. Now the other. Now the legs. You have it!"

Gradually Admetus forced himself forward, and every inch of the way Jason coaxed him along. When he reached the far side, Jason took hold of his arm and helped him up.

Admetus' lip quivered, more from shame than fear. "I wasn't very brave, was I?"

"Neither was I," said Jason. "It's just that nobody was on the other side to notice."

Acastus was next, sliding himself over in a series of swift, determined tugs. When he joined the other two, he was pale and his arms were shaking.

"It's not so bad really, is it?" he declared with an unconvincing smile.

From the other side of the chasm they could hear Lynceus and Idas arguing.

"Look, I'm smaller and lighter than you," Lynceus was saying, "so I should go last. When the rope is tied to that sapling, there's more chance it will support me than you."

His brother disagreed. "I'd still rather trust myself to that scrawny plant than to your puny muscles. Now get going—before I knock you senseless and throw you across."

Lynceus raised a finger and looked ready to argue. Then Idas glowered at him as if he really might knock his brother over the head and fling him over the chasm. So Lynceus shook his head and wrapped himself around the rope. The nimblest of all of the boys, he wriggled quickly along its length like a beetle scuttling across a dirt floor and reached the far side with seeming ease.

Once his brother was safely across, Idas wasted no time looping the rope around the sapling and tying it tightly.

Even from the other side of the chasm, Jason could see that—with the line at full stretch—there was barely enough rope to make a proper knot. He bit his lip. *Will it hold?*

Idas alone did not seem worried. He clambered onto the rope and started tugging himself across, his muscles bulging as he moved forward.

"Not so hard, Idas!" Lynceus cautioned him. "Easy does it."

Idas paid no attention, jerking at the line with all his might. The rope bowed beneath his weight and shook with the force of his exertions.

"He's putting an awful strain on it," said Acastus, tightening his hold on the rope.

Jason watched as the sapling bent and quivered.

The knot! The knot began sliding upward, ripping off strips of dry bark.

Lynceus saw the danger at the same time and gasped, "He's too heavy!"

"The rope is coming loose!" Admetus cried.

"Hurry! Hurry!" shouted Jason. "Not far to go, but hurry!"

"Come on, brother!" Lynceus urged.

Now the rope had caught against a thin branch, and the pressure on the inadequate knot was intense. The sapling bent over so far, some of its thin roots were starting to pull out of the dry ground.

Idas kept dragging himself on with every ounce of strength he had. He was only a few feet from safety when the knot suddenly burst apart.

"Idas!" Lynceus' panic-stricken cry echoed off the chasm walls as the rope came loose and Idas plunged downward. He slid down several hands' breadths, then stopped, gripping the rope as hard as he could right before he collided with the cliff wall.

The four boys on the cliff held tight to their end of the rope, and for a long moment no one spoke.

Under the jarring force of the impact, Idas grunted aloud but did not let go. Then, hand over hand, he dragged himself up the rope, a feat that Jason knew he could never have done himself.

While Acastus and Admetus continued to hold the line, Jason and Lynceus seized Idas by the arms and hauled him up beside them.

As soon as they were all on their feet, Lynceus punched his brother on the chest.

"You great dope!" he exclaimed. "I warned you, but you wouldn't listen!"

Idas ruffled the smaller boy's hair unconcernedly, then gave him a shove that laid him out flat on his back. "Stop making such a fuss," he grumbled. "You sound like Mother."

They all laughed, a sound that was more relief than humor.

Meanwhile, Admetus had pulled up the rest of the rope and wound it into a coil.

Acastus was already making his way uphill. "There's scarcely any light left," he said. "We'd better find a place to make camp. Goat Boy can take the first watch if he thinks it necessary. As for me, I'm ready for a meal."

It took them only a few minutes to find a flat stretch of ground sheltered by a rocky overhang. At this point Jason was too exhausted to challenge Acastus for the leadership. He just followed the prince's orders. Something to eat, somewhere to sleep sounded good to him. He doubted they needed to set a guard.

After a meager supper of bread, goat cheese, and water, they settled themselves down as best they could. They were so weary from the long journey, none of them cared about the lack of bedding.

Acastus' jibes were still stinging Jason, even as he curled into sleep. He thought that if he could only march into Iolcus as rightful king, carried in triumph into the palace, then no one would dare call him a goat boy!

For a brief moment he indulged in a fantasy in which, seated on a golden throne, he issued commands to servants and princes alike. *But,* he thought, suddenly aware of Chiron's voice in his head, *if all you want is power and obedience, how are you any better than the tyrant Pelias?*

Drifting into a heavy sleep, Jason began to dream. In one dream that was both vivid and startling, he saw a woman, her black hair streaked with gray, on her knees before the altar of a dimly lit temple. Her rich robes were disordered and torn, as if she had been fleeing through a forest of thorns. She clutched the altar with both hands like a drowning man with a piece of driftwood. Tears spilled from her eyes.

Suddenly the door to the temple flew open, and in strode a squat, muscular young man, his left cheek stained with a purple mark in the shape of a hoof. In his right hand was a sword that glittered in the light of the many torches lining the walls.

Seizing the weeping woman by the hair, he struck a

single blow that left her at the foot of the altar, a pool of blood spreading out beneath her.

As the killer turned to go, behind the altar a strange light flickered. A stone statue of a goddess—twelve feet tall with offerings laid at its feet—opened its stone eyes. The pale, white brow knotted in anger. The stone hand twitched into life, and the goddess stretched out an arm.

Jason realized to his horror that she was not reaching for the killer, but for him.

He tried to turn and run, but he was fixed to the spot by those glaring stone eyes. The long, cold fingers closed around him, and as he tried to wriggle free, he shook himself awake.

Standing over him was a tall, thin woman, her hair fluttering in the breeze, her thin face shrouded in shadow. He threw up an arm to protect himself, and in that instant she vanished.

Jason sat up and rubbed his eyes, conscious of the dawn. Around him were the sleeping forms of his companions. Idas snored long and low, like a bull grumbling in its sleep. There was no one else to be seen. Nothing unusual except . . . perhaps . . . Jason thought . . . the faintest trace of a smell like rotten meat that was soon carried off by the night breeze.

Had he just imagined the intruder before coming fully awake? There didn't appear to be any danger. Had he been frightened by a nightmare, like a child? And this after managing a real fright, the hand-over-hand trip across the chasm. His fright gave way to fatigue, and he sank back into sleep.

Moments later, he awoke to an uproar.

"Thief!" Acastus was yelling. "One of you is a thief!"

CHAPTER TEN

THE HAUNTED PEAKS

"One of you stole my food pack while I was sleeping." Acastus eyed each of them in turn, his face puffy from anger and sleep.

Idas was leaning on his elbow, bleary-eyed. "What are you talking about?"

"Was it you?" Acastus demanded. "You're the biggest, so you would be the hungriest."

Lynceus was on his feet, taking a swallow from his water skin. "I wouldn't recommend riling Idas before he's had breakfast."

Acastus rounded angrily on the smaller boy. "Was it you, then? You're always sneaking around."

"Why do you think somebody stole your food pack?" Jason asked, trying to sound conciliatory.

"Because it's gone, obviously!" Acastus snapped back. "It was right beside me and now it's gone."

"An animal could have stolen it," Jason suggested.

Acastus waved his arm at the barren mountainside. "What animal?"

"A bird?" said Lynceus.

"Large enough to fly off with my pack? I don't think so."

"Well, it's more likely than one of us stealing it," said Idas, rising slowly to his feet and indulging in a long, satisfying stretch. "Your food pack would have nothing in it that I or Lynceus or any of the others would want."

"Look around if you like," said Jason. "You won't find the pack on any of us."

"You could have eaten the food, then hidden the pack," Acastus insisted.

Jason suddenly noticed that Admetus had not said anything. Normally he would have been enjoying Acastus' annoyance. "You look like there's something on your mind, Admetus."

Admetus shuffled his feet. "Well, I stirred in the night and thought I heard something moving around."

"You mean *someone*," Acastus corrected him.

"No, it was a scraping noise. And there was a funny, rancid smell."

Suddenly Jason remembered the woman bending over him. Surely that had been part of his dream. But the smell . . . He wondered if he should say anything.

Admetus was shaking his head. "I wasn't certain if I was just dreaming, but if something's been stolen . . ." He hesitated and put a hand up to his eyes, scrubbing the sleep from them.

While chewing, Idas said, "We've enough between us to feed Acastus for the rest of our trek. As long as he behaves himself."

Acastus scowled at the joke, but accepted the bread Idas passed to him. The others also contributed to the prince's breakfast—some cheese, some olives. But their gifts did nothing to improve his mood. He was still eyeing them all suspiciously when they set out on the next stage of their journey.

Was there something prowling around our camp? Jason wondered. But it seemed unlikely, that far up the mountainside. And soon he was too busy climbing to think about it any longer.

They were clambering up a series of escarpments that formed a colossal stairway up the mountain slope. Their fingers were raw from clutching at the rough stone, and their arms and legs were scratched and bruised. The sun beating down on their unprotected heads made them dizzy with heat.

They were all too tired even to argue.

That, at least, Jason thought, *is a relief.*

An eerie screech echoed in the distance.

"Did you hear that?" asked Admetus. He stopped and

cocked his head to one side.

"It's just a bird," said Jason. "A hawk of some kind."

"It didn't sound like any hawk I've ever heard," said Lynceus.

"Then it was just the wind whistling through the rocks," Acastus said scornfully. He climbed swiftly ahead to prove he was undaunted by the sound.

Admetus drew up beside Jason and tilted his head in the direction of the northern peaks. "Jason, in my country of Pherae, my people tell tales of these mountains. They call them the Haunted Peaks. Ghosts are supposed to live up here, and sometimes they come down to the valleys and plateaus to steal cattle, sheep, even children."

"I know those stories," Jason admitted. "They tell them to the east of the mountains, too, in Meliboea."

"Do you think any are true?"

Jason laughed. "What would ghosts want with cattle?"

Admetus leaned in close. "To suck the blood out of them. It's the only kind of food they can eat." His voice actually trembled.

"Ghosts!" Idas had overheard and snorted his amusement. "Everybody knows the shades of the dead are in the Underworld, beneath the ground, not up in the mountaintops."

"And we aren't cattle," Jason said. "Or sheep."

"Or children," Acastus added witheringly, "the only ones foolish enough to believe such tales."

It was late in the day when they reached the highest point of their journey so far. The snowy cap of Mount Pelion was visible behind them, while in the sky overhead dark clouds were gathering, making the air heavy with unshed rain.

"Let's stop here and rest a moment," said Jason, dropping to his haunches and catching his breath.

The others all gratefully halted except for Lynceus. "I'm not going to wait around here to get rained on," he said, scrambling on up the slope. "I'll take a look over that next rise and see if there's any shelter."

Jason suddenly became aware of someone breathing at his back. He turned quickly and saw Acastus leaning on his javelin.

"Jason," the prince said quietly, "if you took my food, tell me, and we can settle it now without involving the others."

"I thought we were finished with that, Acastus."

"You and I are not finished with anything."

"Why would I take your pack?"

Acastus narrowed his eyes. "Perhaps to test me, to find out how easy it would be to steal something even more valuable from me."

Jason felt a warning prickle run over his skin. "I don't understand what—"

Suddenly Lynceus' voice rang out above them. "Come and see this! You won't believe it!"

The excitement in his voice was enough to put a fresh

spring in their feet. They clambered up to join him at the top of the rise. Looking down the other side, they saw what it was that had made him cry out.

It was a bowl-shaped hollow about thirty yards across, littered with mounds of crushed branches and dry leaves. Bones—some intact, others cracked open—lay scattered on the ground.

"Look at the skulls!" Lynceus cried, pointing.

Jason was sure he recognized the bones of ox and deer and cattle, as well as skulls of sheep of various sizes. There were horns and antlers and discolored shreds of animal hide.

They descended into the hollow, and Lynceus picked up a broken thighbone. "This has been snapped in two and the marrow sucked out."

"I don't like this . . ." Admetus said.

Jason crouched and picked up the top of a small skull. Broken as it was, it still looked disturbingly human.

"What *is* this place?" Idas wondered. "It looks like a beast's lair, but no bears or wildcats live this high up."

"Or make this big a mess," said Lynceus.

"Or eat this much," added Jason.

"Then it's something else," said Admetus. "Something a lot more dangerous."

"Don't be such a coward," Acastus drawled. "There's nothing to threaten us up here."

"I suppose some kind of bird might nest in the peaks," Jason suggested. "Something very . . ."

"Large?" suggested Idas.

"In that case, why are there no feathers around?" Lynceus objected.

Acastus bent and picked up a length of silver chain that he let dangle from his fingers. Attached to it was a pendant. "It looks like this is the lair of a thief," he declared, "not a bird."

"I don't think so," said Admetus with a nervous shake of his head. "I think this creature, whatever it is, cares only about food. That was probably hanging from the neck of one of its victims."

There was a heartbeat's silence, while they took in the horror of what this implied. Then Lynceus said, "Well, at least one mystery is solved." He was holding up the remains of Acastus' pack. It had been savagely ripped apart but was still recognizable.

"I think Acastus owes us all an apology," said Idas.

Acastus lowered his eyes sullenly. "My suspicions were reasonable under the circumstances," he said stubbornly. "And we still don't know how the pack got up here."

Jason shook his head. It was a waste of time trying to get Acastus to admit he was wrong. They might as well try to force a stream to flow uphill. "Let's get out of here," he said. "The sooner we're away from this place, the better."

Still dangling the pendant in the air, Acastus said, "There may be more treasures here, and it would be stupid to leave them behind."

"I agree with Jason. It's getting dark," put in Admetus. "We should make as much distance as we can before nightfall."

"There's plenty of time," said Acastus coolly. "What is it you're so afraid of? Do you still think there are ghosts up here?"

A shadow flitted across the hollow, accompanied by a strange rustling sound, and a sudden breeze fluttered through Jason's hair. He turned to see what had caused it.

A woman stood on the edge of the hollow. A huge pair of batlike wings was just folding up behind her back. Long yellow hair hung lankly about her shoulders and her gaunt face. She was dressed in a tunic of animal skin tied at the waist with a length of cord.

Jason's recognized her immediately—the woman from his dream. His first impression was of a proud, elemental creature, perhaps a mountain nymph, or even a goddess. Then he saw how thin her arms and legs were, how her tunic was torn and stained and her limbs streaked with dirt. Her feet were broad with thick, curved nails that made them more like claws. Her yellow hair was matted and filthy, and the eyes that glared through the strands flashed with the feral hunger of a wild beast. What faced them was neither woman nor goddess but some sort of monster. And a hungry monster at that.

CHAPTER ELEVEN

WINGED FURY

"I wish I hadn't lost my spear," Idas cried, drawing his sword.

"Maybe . . . she's not dangerous," said Lynceus. "She's just a woman, after all."

At that moment, the winged woman let out an ear-piercing screech, her lips pulled back to expose her teeth. They were sharp and hooked, just right for tearing flesh from bone.

Admetus hefted his spear. "Not *just* a woman, I think."

In response to the winged woman's cry, two more like her plunged out of the clouds and landed at her side. One had hair as black as pitch, the other long red tresses that shimmered like flame. Slowly, as if they had all the time in the world, they folded their great wings behind, then let out snakelike hisses and bared their vicious teeth.

"Who are they?" Idas asked.

"*What* are they?" his brother added.

Each of the women pulled a whip from behind her back. The whips were made of long strands of knotted leather.

Acastus let the silver chain slip through his fingers, and the pendant dropped to the ground with a dull *chink*. "Whatever they are, I don't think they're here to play."

Now the women were uttering a series of strange chirping noises at one another, clearly speaking in some unknown tongue.

"Didn't Chiron tell us about something like this once?" Admetus asked. "Winged women who feed on the bodies of the dead?"

"Of course," Jason said, slapping his forehead. "They're called harpies."

"Well, we're not dead, so they'd better not try anything," Idas reminded them, though his tone was not as defiant as he wanted it to be.

"But this is *their* nest," Lynceus reminded them. "They think *we're* trespassing." He paused. "And we are."

Admetus swallowed hard. "Maybe if we leave quietly . . ."

Keeping his javelin lowered, Jason raised his other

hand to show it was empty and backed slowly away. He hoped the peaceful gesture would appease the harpies. Instead the lead harpy hopped forward in a quick, jerky motion, her head twitching like a bird's. As she hopped, she clicked her hooked teeth together alarmingly.

"She's going to attack!" Idas cried out.

He elbowed Jason aside and struck out with his sword. The bronze point scored a deep cut down the harpy's arm. Black blood splattered the ground.

The harpy shrieked and sprang into the air, her wings unfurling like the sails of a ship. She lashed out at Idas with her clawed foot and caught him in the chin.

Jason tried to get out of the way, but Idas careened into him like a falling tree, knocking them both to the ground. All around them chaos exploded.

The three harpies wheeled about, shrieking madly. The flapping of their wings kicked up billows of dust that enveloped the boys in a choking cloud. Swirling grit stung their eyes and filled their mouths. They coughed and struck out with their weapons, hitting nothing. All the while, the harpies snapped their whips through the murk, lashing the boys on the arms, legs, backs.

Painfully, Jason clambered to his feet. A sword arced over his head to bury itself point first in the ground. Realizing he had lost his javelin in the melee, he turned about trying to find it in the dust, but the red-haired harpy was upon him, raking her talons across his chest.

Jason stumbled back with a howl of pain, his tunic ripped, blood spattering. He drew his sword and slashed out blindly, trying to fend her off.

The harpy pressed forward, jaws snapping, her eyes ablaze with hunger.

Jason had never faced anything so terrifying in his life. Even the centaurs had not frightened him this much. For all that Chiron's cousins could be brutal and unruly, they were still partly human, and that part at least he could understand. But these harpies, though they looked like women, seemed to be goaded only by an animal hunger.

All around him, Jason could see his companions running, ducking, falling. He heard Idas let out a bellow of defiance. Acastus was yelling something about family and honor, his voice thin and shaking.

Then the redheaded harpy darted forward, and her teeth snapped shut barely an inch from Jason's arm. In an unthinking rush of pain and fear, he charged at her, slashing back and forth with his blade, forcing her to retreat. It was fight or die.

Again and again he attacked, driven on by sheer desperate fury. At last the harpy shot upward in a flurry of wings, leaving him choking in a billow of grit.

Admetus staggered past him, the black-tressed harpy dragging him by the hair. Before Jason could help him, he was pitched face first into the dirt. With a screech, the harpy veered away. Groaning and groping about for a weapon, Admetus was a terrible sight. His tunic was shredded and his back crisscrossed with lashes.

Jason knelt beside him and placed a gentle hand on his shoulder. "Here!" he called out, waving his sword over his head. "All of you gather here!"

Lynceus tried to run toward him, but a dry rib bone snapped under his foot and he went tumbling head over heels. Idas appeared, fending off a harpy with his sword. He grabbed his brother by the belt and dragged him to where Jason stood over Admetus.

They looked around for Acastus. One of the harpies had caught the prince's legs in the coils of her whip and had just yanked them from under him. Her talons were poised to rip out his throat.

Jason set an arrow to his bow and hauled back on the string. There was no time for careful aim. He just hoped to hit the monster somewhere. The arrow sang through the air and tore a corner off the harpy's extended wing.

With a shriek of rage, the creature looked up from her victim, giving Acastus the instant he needed to kick loose and scramble over to the other boys.

Startled but unhurt, the harpy came after Acastus, but by now Lynceus had loaded a stone into his sling. Whirling it three times, he let fly and struck the creature on the hand, breaking off one of her talons. The impact made her jerk back and leap into the sky, screeching.

"Good shot!" exclaimed Idas. "Now we're making a fight of it."

Jason passed his sword to Admetus. As if the sword in his hand lent him strength, Admetus stood.

"There's one coming!" Acastus warned.

Jason whirled about, fitting another arrow. "Where?"

"To the north!"

Jason gaped about stupidly. Which way was north? In the bowl of the harpy nest he had lost all sense of direction.

"Duck!" yelled Idas, pushing him down.

The harpy's clawed feet smacked Jason in the back as Acastus lashed out at her with his sword. She wheeled away, squealing and piping to her sisters.

The three winged women now formed a loose circle in the sky overhead and wheeled about the boys. Then they descended to find perches at various points around the edge of the hollow, too far off for Jason or Lynceus to risk one of their precious missiles.

"I've only got about a dozen stones," said Lynceus. "How are you for arrows?"

"About the same," Jason replied. "We'll just have to make every one count."

By now all of the boys were sweating and panting, their skin and clothes smeared with dirt and blood. Dust still drifted through the air and settled bitterly on their tongues.

"I wish it would rain," sighed Admetus, looking up at

the cloudy sky. "At least that would wash off some of this muck."

"Look out!" Idas exclaimed. "They're coming again!"

The harpies had launched themselves into the sky, and now they were sweeping down from three different directions.

Jason jerked his bow this way and that, trying to choose a target. He let fly an arrow at the black-haired harpy, but she swerved aside to dodge it. Lynceus' shot also went wide, and then the harpies were upon them.

Acastus, Idas, and Admetus slashed and stabbed with their blades as whips cracked about them and wicked talons jabbed at their faces. Jason tucked his bow under his arm to keep it safe and stabbed upward with one of his arrows, using it like a dagger.

Suddenly, like leaves blown away by the wind, the harpies raced back to their perches and sat there twitching their heads and licking their wounds.

None of them looked seriously injured.

Worse still, they showed no sign of tiring.

"I don't know how long we can hold them like this," Lynceus said, panting.

"First you wear the enemy down," said Acastus, "and when he falters, you move in for the kill. My father's war counselor taught me that. And it's exactly what they're doing. We can't just stay here."

"If we try to make a run for it, they'll catch us from behind," said Jason.

"I say we make a break for it anyway," said Idas. "At least some of us might get away."

"No," said Jason. "We're not leaving anyone behind. Chiron would want us to stay together."

"Then what's your plan, Jason?" Acastus demanded, his face flushed and angry. "To stand here and die one by one by one?"

CHAPTER TWELVE

THE STORM BREAKS

Jason looked at the others, and he could tell they were all afraid, no matter how much they tried to hide it.

So was he.

His stomach was knotted like a length of rope, and the blood pounded behind his eyes. If he thought about it too much, he might just throw up. Shaking his head, he forced himself to throw off the fear.

"No one is going to die," he said as if he meant it. "Not if we stick together."

"Maybe we can make it to the edge of the hollow and still keep together," said Admetus.

"We'd be going as slow as a tortoise," grumbled Idas.

"That side over there isn't very steep." Lynceus glanced to the right. "We should be able to make it up there without getting stuck."

"Then let's go," said Acastus, impulsively striding off.

The others scurried after him.

"Slow down!" said Jason, grabbing Acastus by the arm. "We're getting separated. Remember what happened with the centaurs. We're no match for them alone, but together we might . . ."

Acastus scowled, but slowed his pace nonetheless.

Step by nervous step they crossed the hollow. Every time there was a flicker of movement from the harpies, the boys pulled up short and pressed together, their weapons thrust out defensively.

The harpies began to hop from one foot to the other, stabbing their claws toward the sky as if signaling. Then one suddenly pumped her wings and took to the air. She soared overhead, then plunged downward like a plummeting hawk, to land directly in front of them. She leaned down, snatched up a rock, and flung it, cracking Idas in the shin.

For an instant, Idas seemed to buckle.

"Up, Idas, up!" Jason cried, jerking him up by the arm.

Idas winced. "That'll make a fine purple bruise."

"By the gods!" Admetus exclaimed. "They learn fast." He pointed.

All three of the harpies had now scooped up armfuls of rocks. Taking to the air, they hovered ahead of the boys and, with horrendous screeches, began pelting them with stones.

The rain of stones forced the boys to fall back.

"Damn them to the blackest pit in Tartarus!" Idas roared, as much in rage as in pain.

Slowly they were forced back into the very center of the hollow, where they crouched with their arms up to ward off the stone missiles.

All the while, the harpies shrieked and hooted and twittered, which sounded a great deal like mocking laughter. Then they returned to their perches and watched their victims with hungry eyes.

"If they're mad at us for trespassing, why don't they just let us go or chase us off?" said Admetus, his voice almost a sob. "Why are they keeping us here?"

"Because they're hungry," Idas said darkly.

"Hungry?" Admetus echoed bleakly.

"Look around, cousin," Acastus said. "They'll eat anything." His usual mocking tone was gone. "And now they've got us here, they don't intend to let us go."

"Then there's no choice," said Idas with gloomy determination. "We have to run for it. Each of us will have to trust to his own speed. If we each go in a different direction, at least some of us will get away. Some is better than none."

"All is better yet." Jason realized that they were not listening to him.

"If only we had a way to distract them," said Lynceus.

Jason suddenly remembered Acastus' stolen pack. The harpy who had sneaked into camp had come to steal food, not to prey on the boys. At least not then. He clapped his hands together, which got everyone's attention. "We can use the food."

"Food? You mean our food?" Acastus looked dubious.

"Yes. Use their hunger against them. Given the chance of a meal that doesn't fight back, my guess is that they'll go for it at once."

"Your guess?" Acastus shook his head.

"Have a better idea?" Jason asked. "Throw it far enough away from us and they'll chase after it."

"I think Jason's right," Admetus said.

"I do, too," agreed Idas.

"All of the food?" Lynceus did not seem so sure.

"That's the only way we can be certain of delaying them long enough for us to get away," Jason told them.

"And what are we supposed to live on then?" asked Acastus.

"Would you rather go hungry or be a meal for somebody else?"

"You're right, Jason," Lynceus said, "but couldn't we keep just a little back? For a snack?"

"Too risky," said Jason decisively. "We're going to need as big a lead as we can get." *And even that,* he thought, *may not be big enough.*

He gathered all the remaining bread, meat, and cheese into one pack, and with his knife cut slits in the sides, just enough so that the food could be easily spilled. He left the flap open. Then he handed the pack to Idas. "Throw it as far as you can," he said, "over that way." He pointed to the way they had come.

Idas gripped the pack, all the while watching the harpies. They were still hopping from foot to foot, waiting for another opportunity to attack. "Now?"

"Now!" the boys all said as one.

Idas swung his brawny arm, once, twice, then let go. The pack shot upward, then curved down toward the ground. When it landed, it spilled its contents in all directions.

The harpies instantly burst into the air with excited squawks, then raced for the food on beating wings. As soon as they landed, they jabbed and scratched one another in a frenzy of hunger, not wanting to share even the tiniest morsel.

"Go!" Jason shouted.

Lynceus was already away, but Idas soon overtook him with his long strides. Jason pulled ahead of Admetus with Acastus just in front of him. Then he was ahead.

How long will the food hold them? Jason wondered. *How long before they notice that their live prey has fled?* He didn't dare look back. The least delay could mean death. He just kept running, never minding the dried bones cracking and crumbling underfoot.

They reached the far side of the hollow, and Jason felt the breath hot in his chest, his legs trembling with fatigue and fear. He was certain the others felt the same.

Suddenly there was a horrifying flutter of wings behind him, above him. A foul breeze washed over him, and the guttural chatter of the harpies drummed in his ears.

Without turning to look, Jason forced himself on. There was the snap of a whip and something clipped his ear; then he was over the edge, racing down the side of the mountain without even glancing at the way ahead. He stumbled and rolled over the bumpy ground, colliding with a shriveled tree.

Looking up, he saw the golden-haired harpy above him, her wings spread out, her horrid teeth bared. Then a shock of light exploded across the sky. There was a deafening boom of thunder, and a wall of rain crashed out of the clouds, hitting the earth like a waterfall.

Jason was drenched in the sudden downpour. It filled his eyes and trickled down his throat. Another sheet of lightning ripped across the sky, illuminating the harpy. She was twisting about in the air the way a drowning sailor is rolled in a terrible sea. The storm buffeted her about, the raindrops rattling like a shower of pebbles on her outstretched wings. Soon she lost sight of her victim, and the gusts of rain began beating her back to her lair.

Clambering to his feet, Jason felt the ground slick and muddy beneath him. He slid down the slope, putting as much distance as possible between himself and the ravenous monsters. He tried to call to the others, but his voice was lost in the roar of the rain.

Pausing to check his bow, he found it miraculously undamaged. However, still wary of an attack by the harpies, he took out an arrow, set it on the string, and held it ready. Picking his way from rock to rock to avoid falling in the mud, he wound his way around toward the north, alert for any shelter from the storm.

To his relief the lightning revealed the dark outline of a cave entrance. Hardly daring to believe, Jason hurried toward it, doing his best to keep his balance.

He stopped at the entrance and froze. Even over the din of the rain, he was sure he could hear something moving inside. He drew the string of the bow back sharply and stepped inside.

Immediately he felt the point of a bronze blade pricking his throat.

Lightning lit up the cave, and he saw Acastus staring at him down the length of his outstretched arm and the straight edge of his sword. Jason's arrowhead, with all the pent-up force of the bowstring gathered behind it, was poised only inches from the prince's heart.

"Jason!" Acastus breathed. Then he asked, "Where are the others? Are they safe?"

"I don't know," Jason replied. "I lost sight of them in the storm."

His arm was starting to ache under the strain of holding back his bowstring, but some instinct told him not to relax.

"The harpies?" Acastus asked. His sword point had not wavered by the least fraction.

"I think they're gone," Jason answered, both arms shaking.

There was a long silence, broken only by the battering of the rain outside the cave.

"Shouldn't we lower our weapons now?" Jason suggested at last. His throat was burning, and it was hard to get the words out.

Acastus let out a long, low breath. "I suppose we should."

But his sword didn't move. And *his* arm was not shaking.

CHAPTER THIRTEEN

THE ANGER OF HERA

Raindrops from his wet hair and sweat trickled down Jason's face, dampening his parched lips. He could not tell if the heart he heard beating was his own or Acastus'.

A yelp from behind made him start. His fingers almost slipped from the bowstring. A tremor passed down Acastus' arm, and the sword point tickled Jason's chin.

"Oh, it's only you, Jason!" gasped Lynceus' voice. "And you, Acastus. Thank the gods! I thought it might be harpies—or something even worse. Hoi, what's going on?"

Slowly Jason let the point of his arrow drop and eased off the pressure on the bowstring. As he did so, Acastus lowered his sword.

"For a moment we thought the same thing," Acastus

said. "Harpies or something worse. But we're just friends here." He smiled, but there was little warmth in it.

"Well, friends," Lynceus said, "move aside and make some room for me." He squeezed past them into the shelter of the cave. "Not much room in here, is there?" he observed. "Hardly bigger than a hen coop."

"Better than a harpy's nest," Acastus said.

Jason gave a grunt of agreement, then addressed the two boys. "Give me your water skins. There's no point in wasting this rain."

While the other two dried off in the cave, Jason went out into the downpour and held out the skins until the rain had topped them up. He was still tense from his confrontation with Acastus, still wary that a harpy might find him again and attack.

But the longer he stood out in the rain unharmed, the more time he had to think. He knew Acastus didn't like him, but surely he didn't want to harm him. Or was it that Acastus was afraid of him?

He took the water skins back inside and passed them to the others.

Lynceus lofted his water skin in salute and took a grateful swallow. "Well, we may starve in this coop, but at least we won't die of thirst." He looked out into the rain and frowned. "I hope Idas is all right. He'd never admit it, but he needs me to look after him. I should go out there. . . ."

"I'm certain he's fine," said Jason, wishing that he were really sure. "We don't dare go back."

"I understand," Lynceus said, but the hand holding the water skin shook, and his eyes were shining with unshed tears.

Acastus had not spoken. He was staring gloomily at the floor.

"What are you brooding about?" Jason asked.

"My first battle," Acastus replied sourly, "and all we did was run away. We didn't even kill one of those monsters."

"I'm not sure they can be killed," Lynceus said with a shudder.

"You fought bravely," Jason told the prince, "as bravely as any of us. There was no victory to be won today, only survival."

"And what do you know about bravery, Goat Boy?" Acastus burst out. "Nobody expects you to be a warrior or a hero. You can tend your goats and pick your berries and nobody thinks any the worse of you for it. You should be glad of that and stay where you belong."

If he had not known better, Jason could have sworn that for an instant the prince had sounded jealous.

"Jason's shown more courage and wits than any of us," said Lynceus. "Without him we would never have made it this far."

"You and I have made it, but what about Ademetus and Idas? Our *guide* has not served them so well."

"We can still hope that they are alive and well and sheltered as we are," Jason said.

"Is hope all you have to offer, Goat Boy?" Acastus sneered and turned his back to them.

Lynceus offered Jason a weak smile and moved away from them, mumbling something about sleep. Then he lay down and tucked his head under his arm, choking back a sob.

"We should *all* get some sleep," said Jason. "Tomorrow we have to find the others and climb down off this mountain."

No one bothered to answer him.

They made themselves as comfortable as they could in their cramped quarters. Acastus backed up to Lynceus, as if being anywhere near Jason would prove catching, like a disease.

Jason folded his arms under his head and wriggled about until there weren't too many bumps poking into his ribs. He was so exhausted that sleep came quickly in spite of everything.

He had no idea what hour of the night it was when he began to stir. He only knew that he was aware of an unknown presence in the cave with them.

Keep still and play dead, he thought. *Be ready to grab the advantage of surprise.*

Without shifting his position he slowly opened his eyes. All he could see was the cave wall in front of him.

Inch by inch he gradually turned his head toward the entrance.

What he saw made him jump up and step back.

Standing there, lit by some unknown light, was a beautiful, majestic woman. She seemed too tall to be standing upright in this tiny place, yet she did not crouch. She had a high, pale brow, above which a jeweled diadem crowned her black ringlets. Her eyes were large and dark as the night sky. Draped over her shoulders was a cloak made of peacock feathers that flashed and gleamed like a thousand multicolored eyes.

For all her beauty, she was as frightening as the harpies—yet there was something familiar about her.

"Jason, son of Aeson." Her voice filled the cave like a trumpet blast.

Jason was astonished at the power in her voice, and even more astonished that the others didn't waken. He nodded dumbly.

"Do you know who I am?" she demanded.

"I think I should," Jason replied hesitantly.

"Then think harder." Her voice, though cold, had a hint of humor.

He closed his eyes and thought hard. "I think . . . I saw a statue of you last night in a dream."

"A dream *I* sent you," she intoned. "Thus do we prepare mortals for our coming."

His eyes sprang open. "You're one of the gods of Olympus."

The goddess's eyes flared like pools of oil catching fire. She said angrily, "Not *one* of the gods, mortal. I am Hera, bride of all-powerful Zeus, queen of all the gods."

Startled by her sudden anger, Jason pushed backward till he was up against the stone wall. But it was farther away than he had thought. Then he realized that the walls had expanded around Hera, forming a huge vaulted cavern, the sides of which reflected her gleaming peacock cloak.

Chiron had warned him that the gods demanded awe and respect and despised cowardice. He was already awed to the point of terror. He would try respect as well, and maybe that would disguise his fear. Drawing himself up, Jason made a respectful bow.

"I'm honored, mighty queen," he said. "But why should you want to visit me? Here in this cave? I am no one of importance."

"You are important to me, Jason," Hera said. As she spoke he could see himself, small and fragile, reflected in the polished blackness of her eyes. "Did you think that storm"—and she flung her left arm wide to encompass all that was outside the cave entrance—"came from nowhere? It was I who rescued you from the harpies."

"I d-didn't know." Jason was shocked to find himself stammering. "But if it was you, I thank you, mighty one."

"You have a great destiny ahead of you," Hera continued. "That is why I have watched over you. But to claim what is yours by birth, you must first kill the prince—Acastus!"

The words echoed about the cave like a crash of thunder. Jason's ears rang with the sound.

He bowed his head and then looked up again. "I've no reason to kill Acastus," he said quietly. "He's done nothing to me." Though he could not forget the look in Acastus' face and the sword that did not shake in his hand.

"Aeson's son, it is your fate to claim the throne of Iolcus, the throne Acastus believes is his by right." Hera's face was at once beautiful and terrible.

"Why does my fate matter so much to you, O great queen?"

"Not your fate, Jason. What matters to me is the fate of Pelias, Acastus' father. All that I can do to bring about his downfall I will. Do you recall the dream I sent you last night?"

Jason nodded. "The woman in the temple, and the man who killed her," he whispered.

"That dream was a true one. That man was Pelias." Hera's lips curled in contempt. "The woman was Sidero, who had cruelly mistreated Pelias' mother. She fled to my alter and sought sanctuary there, but Pelias slew her anyway. I would have struck him down there and then for such a dishonor, but Poseidon, the sea god, stayed my hand. Pelias was under his protection."

"Ah." Jason shook his head.

"We gods must not war among ourselves. My husband, Zeus, brother of Poseidon, has decreed it. And so I need a human instrument to carry out my revenge." She loomed over Jason, seeming to grow even larger.

"Me?" Jason's voice squeaked, and he pressed back hard against the rocks.

"I have watched you these many years, Jason. I have seen Chiron train you in the arts of combat and hunting. *You* are the weapon I have been waiting for to visit my vengeance on Pelias and his house. In a few more years you will go to Iolcus, kill Pelias, and take the throne that is yours by right."

Jason was horrified at the thought. The throne might be his by right, but would right be served by murder? He knew what Chiron would say. "No, there *must* be a way to become the king without killing."

Hera's laughter was brittle and mocking. "How little you understand your own mortal world."

"Perhaps I could perform some feat of daring instead," Jason said, "something that will win me the respect of the people of Iolcus. If they choose me as king, Pelias will be forced to stand aside and then—"

"Only a fool puts his trust in the mob," said Hera. "You can injure Pelias now by killing his heir. That way he is but half a king. Easier to dispose of later."

Jason swallowed and tried once again to meet Hera's gaze. "Acastus may make fun of me, goddess. He may challenge me and call me names. But that's not reason enough to kill him. "

"I command it. Is that not reason enough?" Her voice was cold.

"I'm no murderer, great one." He held up his hands to her, pleading.

"I saw him draw his sword on you. I saw how strong his arm is. He will not always be stopped by others. Kill him now, while you have the chance." Hera's voice was pitiless. "Pitch his body down the mountainside. Lynceus will not awake and see it, I promise you. I can even make him forget Acastus was ever here in the cave. Everyone will assume the harpies caught up with him." She smiled.

Jason turned his head away, unable to face Hera's terrible gaze. "No. Never."

Hera's whole body was now ablaze with a crimson light. It seemed as if the very walls of the cave were catching fire.

"If you do not kill him now, he will surely try to kill you."

"I can't do it."

"Spurn my advice and you may find you spurn my favor," she cried. "No one lasts long, young mortal, without the gods' protection!"

Jason fell to his knees. "I honor you, goddess, but I

can't kill a companion in cold blood." Now he dared to glance up at her.

"I will remember that," she said. In the fiery light her face was a mixture of anger and something else. He hoped it was understanding.

There was a sound like a thunderclap, and the goddess was gone.

CHAPTER FOURTEEN

THE MOUNTAIN WAKES

Daylight spilled through the cave entrance, and everything was back to normal. Jason rubbed his eyes.

"Is it morning already?" Lynceus groaned, rubbing his belly. "Yes, it must be. My stomach's demanding breakfast."

Acastus sat up, stretched his arms, and stared at Jason, who still had his back pressed to the wall. "What's wrong with you, Goat Boy? You look like you've seen a ghost."

"No, not a ghost," said Jason. "Just . . . a bad dream." But he knew that wasn't true. On the stone floor at his feet, he could see the broken feather, though neither of the others had noticed it. He put his foot over it.

"When the days are as rough as ours have been, I

don't see the point in bad dreams," said Lynceus. "I was dreaming about soft beds, warm fires, honey cakes, and roast boar." He hugged himself tightly. "With my brother nearby."

"Well, it's water for breakfast and that's all," said Acastus bluntly. "Unless one of you two dreamers went out hunting during the night."

When Lynceus and Acastus stepped outside the cave, Jason bent over and picked up the broken feather. Its lustrous greens and purples gleamed like jewels. Had Hera left it for him on purpose? And if so, was it a promise or a threat?

Stashing the feather safely inside his tunic, he joined the others in the open air.

The sky had cleared to a brilliant blue. To the north they could see the snowy peak of Mount Ossa, its lower slopes no more than a day's march away. Far beyond Ossa, Jason knew, lay the third of the great peaks, Mount Olympus itself, the home of the gods. He wondered uneasily if Hera was there now, watching him from her throne. The peacock feather he had stuffed down the front of his tunic felt warm against his skin.

A promise, he thought.

As they started down the slope, Lynceus raised his head and yelled, "Ho, Idas! Admetus! Where are you?"

Acastus silenced him with a shove. "Not so loud, you fool! You'll bring the harpies down on us again."

Lynceus looked to Jason. "Do you think so?"

"I don't know," said Jason, "but it's best to be careful."

"If we don't shout, how will we find them?"

"We may *never* find them," Acastus said bluntly.

Lynceus thought for a moment, then said, "I know! When we were boys, Idas and I used bird calls to signal each other. I remember once when we were raiding our neighbor's orchard, I stood lookout, and if I saw anybody coming, I made a noise like a thrush to warn him."

"You were stealing apples?" Jason exclaimed.

"Well, we weren't old enough to steal cattle." He cupped his hands around his mouth and made a low, warbling noise that carried far across the mountainside. When he had finished, he cocked an ear, but there was no answering call.

"Come on," said Jason. "I'm sure they'll turn up."

Acastus shook his head but said nothing.

They made their way down the mountain, finding what trails they could. Every few minutes, Lynceus stopped to let out a bird call.

"Come on, Idas, answer me," he muttered. "I know you're all right."

"I believe that, too," Jason told him, putting a hand on Lynceus' shoulder. It was well meant, but the boy shook the hand off and moved away, though not before

Jason saw how he was fighting back tears.

Then Lynceus cupped his hands around his mouth again, but before he could call out, he lost his footing on some loose shale and went slithering down the slope—straight into the arms of Idas, who had just rounded a bend a few yards below. Admetus was with Idas, and the other boys scurried down to join them.

"I *thought* it was you making that ridiculous noise," Idas told his brother.

"If you heard me, why didn't you answer?" Lynceus demanded. "You know how to make the call." The tears were running down his cheeks, but now—it seemed—such a display no longer mattered.

"I didn't see any point in both of us making fools of ourselves," Idas answered in deadpan fashion.

The other boys started giggling, then fell back and erupted into gales of laughter. It was a relief to find something funny after all they'd been through. None of them gave a thought to the harpies.

"Where *were* you?" Lynceus asked when they'd quieted at last.

"We found a cleft in the rocks that gave us some shelter," Idas replied.

"Some, but not much," Admetus added.

"At least we're all safe," said Jason, "and from now on we only have to go downhill."

Admetus suddenly looked up at the sky. It was a clear

blue without a single cloud. "Do you think the harpies will come after us again?"

"The rain will have washed away our tracks and our scent," said Idas. He sounded more hopeful than sure.

"They've probably forgotten all about us," Jason reassured them, "and gone in search of easier prey." He didn't mention Hera's hand in their escape, but he could feel the peacock feather warm against his chest.

They had not gone much farther when from somewhere above them came a deep, threatening rumble.

"Not more thunder!" Lynceus groaned.

Jason turned and looked up. The sky was still a clear blue. "It's not thunder." He pointed.

On the slopes above them, the mountain itself was coming to life, the earth and mud shifting like a blanket being tossed off by a slumbering giant. Great boulders were slipping out of place, crashing and banging off one another as they rolled downhill. They collided with other stones farther down, sweeping the smaller stones along in a growing tide.

"Rock slide!" Acastus cried.

Already loose pebbles were rolling past their feet, and they could feel the mountain shake beneath them.

"We've got to get out of here!" cried Admetus. He began to run downward, away from the danger.

Lynceus tugged urgently at his brother's tunic.

"Come on! This isn't the kind of enemy you can fight!"

They fled in a wild panic, sprinting and jumping, but it was hard to run without taking a fall on this steep, uncertain ground. The rumbling behind them grew louder, the bouncing stones growing larger, like wild dogs snapping at their heels.

As he drew even with Admetus, Jason saw Lynceus and Idas disappearing from view off to his right. Acastus was racing away to his left, bounding over obstacles, as startled as a deer.

"We'll never get away!" Admetus gasped.

Some wordless sense of danger made Jason turn his head. Out of the corner of his eye he saw a boulder the size of a haystack bearing down on the two of them.

"Look out!" he yelled, shoving Admetus out of the path.

He himself veered left, but the boulder clipped his shoulder as it crashed past. The impact tossed Jason headlong down the slope, and he tumbled and bumped over the rough ground.

At last he rolled to a stop and scrambled onto his hands and knees. Looking ahead, he almost screamed out loud. Less than ten feet away was the edge of a precipice. He stood and turned, trying to get clear, but he was no sooner up than a tide of earth and stones whipped his legs out from under him and swept him toward his doom.

He tried to dig in his heels, but still he skidded

downward, unable to stop. His feet shot off the edge, and with a final despairing cry he was flung out into empty space. Below him a sheer drop plunged all the way down to the foot of the mountain.

Then—from out of nowhere—someone grabbed his arm.

A horrid wrench jolted Jason's shoulder. Numb from shock, he hung there, helpless as a fish on a line. Looking up, he saw Acastus staring down at him.

There was a ledge jutting out from the mountain-side about five feet below the cliff's edge. Acastus had taken refuge here ahead of him. Now the prince had one hand jammed into a tight crevice to hold himself in place. With the other hand he had a firm hold on Jason's left arm.

A cataract of stones burst over the cliff edge and scattered through the air, peppering Jason like pecking birds.

"Pull me up!" Jason yelled. "Pull me up!"

Acastus kept his grip but left Jason hanging. The veins bulged on his outstretched arm, and his face was flushed with the effort.

"What's the matter with you?" Jason demanded, his voice sounding shrill in his own ears.

"I know who you are, Jason," Acastus said in a dull voice.

"What?" Jason thought for a dreadful moment the prince had gone mad.

"You're Aeson's son. I overheard Chiron saying so."

A cold chill ran down Jason's back. "I swear I knew nothing about it till that moment," he said hoarsely. "I always thought I was an orphan."

"Well, now you know differently." Acastus sounded cold and determined.

More rocks came spilling over the edge. Acastus was sheltered by the overhang, but Jason took a knock to his leg.

"It doesn't matter, Acastus," Jason pleaded. "Not to me."

Gritting his teeth against the strain of supporting Jason's weight, Acastus cried, "It matters to *me*! If my father had known about you, he would have killed you years ago."

Jason's insides turned to water. He understood now why Acastus had held a sword to his throat. And now, if the prince let him fall to his death, no one would ever know. They would all assume he'd been swept away by the rock slide.

Through the red haze of panic, Jason tried to think clearly, to keep his voice calm. "We've helped each other this far. All the dangers we've come through together—does that mean nothing to you?"

Acastus' mouth twisted. "I can't think about that now. I have to think about what comes after. I've been raised from birth to be a king, to rule Iolcus. That is my birthright, and your existence threatens it, Goat Boy."

Jason looked down, saw the terrible drop, saw the

jagged rocks waiting below, sharp as harpies' teeth. And still he dangled. *Why? Why?*

For all his ruthless talk, Acastus had not yet summoned the nerve to kill him in cold blood. That was the only hopeful sign.

But cold blood or hot, all Acastus had to do was loosen his grip by a fraction. And if he didn't do it on purpose, fatigue would soon do it for him.

The peacock feather was a flame against Jason's skin. He could hear Hera's mocking laughter in the rumble of the landslide. It seemed she'd been right after all. He should have killed Acastus when he'd had the chance.

CHAPTER FIFTEEN

THE VALLEY OF DEATH

Jason squeezed his eyes tight shut and fought to keep his voice steady, ignoring the pain in his arm, the heat of the feather at his breast. "If we don't catch up with the centaurs," he said slowly, clearly, "there will be no birthright. Not for you, not for anyone."

"What are you talking about?" Acastus said. "What's so important about those jars?"

Jason had no choice now but to tell the whole truth.

"The jars contain Gorgon's blood. One of them—the red jar—holds a poison deadly enough to kill every man, woman, and child in Iolcus, maybe even in the whole of Thessaly."

He could feel Acastus tense up, the fingers digging into his flesh.

"I've heard that tale," the prince said. "Perseus and the blood of Medusa. Do you mean to tell me that the deadliest poison in all the world is now in the hands of those undisciplined brutes?"

"Yes."

Acastus took a deep breath. "By the gods . . ." The hand holding Jason shook.

Jason was careful in what he said next. It was, he figured, the only chance he would get. "Acastus, isn't stopping the centaurs more important than arguing over who should sit on the throne?"

"You're right, Jason. I have to stop them." Acastus sounded thoughtful. "It's my duty. *My* duty, not yours." His fingers started to loosen.

"Think, Acastus!" Jason urged him. "Are you so certain you can beat those creatures without me that you would risk the lives of all your people?"

There was a pause that seemed to last an eternity. Pain was running down Jason's arm like threads of fire. A rock the size of his head clipped the edge of the cliff and flew off into space, horribly close.

Then Acastus gave a strenuous heave and hauled Jason up. Hooking his foot over the ledge, Jason scrambled up beside the prince and lay there gasping for breath. He wondered if his left arm would ever work again.

"Five of us are few enough as it is," Acastus said grimly. "You have shown courage."

Jason used his other arm to wipe the sweat from his brow. "Whatever your father might think, Acastus, we don't have to be enemies."

"Yes, we do." Acastus' voice was flat. "It's our destiny. As our fathers were enemies, so are we. Once those jars are recovered, then we will settle this matter honorably, warrior against warrior, sword against sword." As he spoke, his fingers drifted to the gold amulet about his neck.

"Not *everything* needs to be settled with swords and with blood," said Jason.

Acastus leaned back with his eyes closed, as though recovering from a terrible struggle. "The fact that you can say such a thing shows that you have no honor, Goat Boy. Courage, yes. But not honor. Without honor, you can't possibly be a king."

Jason, too, closed his eyes. He tried to remember what Chiron had said about honor. But all he could think of was how thankful he was to be alive.

Gradually the rock slide subsided, a last stone rattling down the cliff face. Then there came a silence as vast as the sea.

Jason hardly dared to stir. The ledge was so narrow that a careless move could still send either one of them toppling to his death. He opened his eyes.

Acastus was now staring off into the distance, lost in his own thoughts. Jason wondered if he was relieved to have been given a reason not to commit murder, not to do the cruel thing his father would have chosen to do. There was no reading his face, though, and Jason leaned back against the cliff face.

"Hallo!" boomed a voice. "Hallo! Are any of you there?"

"Here!" Jason called back. "We're down here!"

He moved closer to Acastus and whispered, "Don't tell the others about my being Aeson's son."

"Don't worry," said Acastus. "This is just between the two of us."

Idas' face appeared over the cliff edge above them. "What a pretty spot to build a nest." He laughed.

Lynceus peeked over his brother's shoulder. "I was afraid we'd seen the last of you."

Craning his neck, Acastus looked up. "How did you two escape that rock fall?"

"We managed to take refuge in a small stand of trees," Lynceus said. "I don't know about Admetus, though. We haven't found him yet."

Idas lay down on his belly and stretched out his arm. "Come on. Give me your hand."

For a moment Jason hesitated. His left arm was still so sore, he doubted he could reach that high. So Acastus was pulled up first. But with all three boys helping, Jason was soon standing beside them.

Lynceus peered down at the dizzying drop. "I think we'd better find another way to get to the bottom."

"First we need to look for Admetus," said Jason.

Acastus shrugged. "Crushed to death? Or over the edge, like you, perhaps."

"We *have* to look," Jason insisted. Then he added, "Remember, even five is few enough."

"Few enough for what?" Lynceus asked.

Acastus gave him an angry look, a warning to be quiet.

"Few enough to fight those centaurs, idiot," Idas answered.

Smiling but silent, Jason turned away.

The four boys spread out over the mountainside shouting Admetus' name, no longer worried about the harpies. Minute after minute they called, to no answer.

Jason was beginning to suspect Acastus was right. They were lucky enough that four had managed to stay alive through that rock slide. Five would be a miracle.

He touched the top of his tunic, felt the peacock feather warm beneath his hand.

Just then he heard a call.

Raising a hand for silence, in case it was a harpy, he listened carefully.

There it was again: a long, drawn-out groan. Not a harpy, then.

"It's coming from over here," cried Lynceus, darting to the spot.

The others gathered around a crack in the ground, about three feet wide, filled with dirt and rock. Something was stirring under the rubble.

Acastus drew his sword. "Watch out! This could be anything!"

A hand thrust up from the fissure.

"Admetus!" Jason exclaimed.

"You can't know that," Acastus warned.

But the others ignored him and began digging away the rocks as Jason grabbed the hand. When enough rubble was cleared away, he dragged the young prince out of the hole.

Admetus stood shakily, coughing and blinking, still holding his spear, which—miraculously—was whole.

"I fell in," he explained, rubbing the grime from his face. "I suppose the bigger rocks bounced over me."

Idas gave a hearty laugh and clapped Admetus on the back. "The favor of the gods must be with you, Admetus."

"You don't suppose it was the harpies that started that rock slide," Lynceus wondered aloud, "you know—to get back at us."

"I don't think they're that devious," said Acastus. "Most likely it was caused by the heavy rain loosening the earth."

"That's probably it," Jason agreed. But he couldn't help remembering Hera's feather, hot under his fingers, and he wondered if the rock slide had been a sign of her displeasure.

As soon as Admetus had had a long drink of water, they set off again, quickly reaching the lower slopes. Here trees and plants grew thickly, some well thorned, others with velvety leaves. The boys could hear small animals scurrying through the undergrowth.

Jason drew in a deep breath. The air was sweeter here.

Finding some berries, Admetus shared them around. Washed down with a swallow of water, the berries restored all their spirits, but Idas was still complaining of hunger.

"My stomach tells me that my throat has felt the knife," he said.

"Shhh!" cautioned Lynceus. "Something's coming."

On the slope below, a wild goat, white with little nubbins for horns, suddenly appeared and began cropping the shrubs.

"Now that's more like it," whispered Idas, licking his lips.

Admetus stood slowly and raised his spear. He was still battered and weary, and his arm trembled.

"Leave this to me," said Idas, taking the spear from him.

He fixed a keen eye on his target and drew back his arm. The spear flew straight and fast, piercing the little goat right through the middle. With a whoop, the boys ran down to where their prize lay, and Idas finished the animal off with a stroke of his sword.

They had all been trained by Chiron in how to gut a kill and strip away the beast's hide. They were well adept at starting a fire with kindling and flints. Soon they were feasting on roasted goat meat. It was juicy, and though the beast was small, there was still plenty of meat to go around.

Idas sighed and rubbed his stomach. Then he belched.

"Loud enough," Lynceus said, "to summon the gods!"

"This reminds me of my father's last victory feast," said Acastus, wiping some grease from his chin. "I ate so much I thought I would burst."

Admetus grinned. "If you burst here, you can clean up the mess yourself!"

"You're one to talk, Admetus," said Lynceus. "You still look like something that just crawled out of a grave."

Admetus held up his hands and waggled his fingers. "I am the ghostly prince of the mountains. Look on my remains and tremble."

Everybody laughed.

Admetus flung a bare bone at them, and Lynceus ducked with a chuckle.

Jason couldn't remember when he had last tasted anything as good as the goat's meat. Even their plain water seemed suddenly as intoxicating as wine.

They were all reclining on the ground, almost stupefied by the meal, when Acastus looked to the west, where the sun was beginning to sink. "We need to keep moving while we still have the light," he said, suddenly serious. "The longer we delay, the more time the centaurs have to plan their mischief."

"Couldn't we just digest a little longer?" Idas pleaded, sprawling on the grass.

"Acastus is right," said Admetus. "Who knows what those brutes are up to?"

Acastus and Jason exchanged a quick, secretive glance.

"I agree," Jason said. "We've fed well. Now we need to eat up the miles." He stood, and the two princes stood with him.

Lynceus jumped up and gave his brother a kick. "Come on, greedy guts! Your belly can do its work while you walk."

Descending through the darkening air into the valley of Hecla, they scouted for a place to camp. Suddenly Lynceus let out a low whistle and signaled the others to be quiet.

"There," he said, "just past those trees."

Jason peered through the branches. "What is it?"

"Men. Six of them."

Idas crept up to look as well. "They're lying on the ground. Are they asleep?"

Lynceus swallowed. "I don't think so. It's too early to be abed."

They approached cautiously, using whatever cover they could find, their weapons at the ready. The closer they got, the more obvious it became that the six men were not sleeping. Their bodies were contorted, heads cracked open with clubs, blood everywhere. Broken spears and bent shields littered the ground. The wreckage of at least three chariots had also been scattered across the valley. There was no sign of the horses.

"Soldiers from Iolcus," said Acastus, a catch in his voice. "See the crest on that shield."

Jason bent to examine the ground. "Look at these hoofprints." He pointed. "Centaurs did this."

"Why are your father's men up here?" Admetus asked.

"I don't know," Acastus answered bitterly.

Idas and Lynceus had gone over to a clump of bushes. They called to the others.

"Over here," Idas cried, his normally ruddy face pale. "You haven't seen the worst of it yet."

CHAPTER SIXTEEN

ALCESTIS

Idas was standing over another body, but this one was different. He was dressed in the robes of a priest, and he did not look as if he had been in any sort of a battle. But for all that, he was just as dead as the soldiers.

The priest's face was contorted into a hideous grimace, and his skin was stained a livid purple. His arms were twisted and shriveled like the branches of a withered tree, the fingers curled into claws. Huge rents ran down the front of his robe where he had obviously torn at it himself, for there were broken threads under his fingernails.

The boys gathered round. Admetus muttered a prayer for the protection of the gods.

Acastus ground his teeth and slashed the air with his

sword. "I knew this good man," he said. "Before I left Iolcus, he made a sacrifice on the steps of the palace to ensure that the gods protected me on my journey to Mount Pelion."

"It looks like he died in agony," Admetus said, closing the man's eyes.

"But there's no sign of any wound, no blood," Lynceus observed.

Jason shuddered but said nothing. He was afraid he knew what had killed the priest.

"There are more of them over there." Idas pointed.

A few yards away there were three more dead men, all disfigured like the first.

"What could possibly have turned them that awful color?" Admetus asked.

"It's the poison," Acastus said flatly.

"What poison?" asked Lynceus.

"The poison we've come to retrieve for Chiron. Jason can tell you about it."

There was a long silence as all the boys turned to stare at Jason.

Finally Lynceus exclaimed, "That's what's in those jars the centaurs stole."

Jason took a deep breath, thinking: *Forgive me, Chiron, but they have to know.* Then he said, "One of the jars contains a deadly poison, true."

"The poison's the blood of Medusa," said Acastus. "Gorgon's blood."

The boys were struck silent.

Jason nodded. "In the other jar is a healing potion."

"It doesn't look like Nessus and his friends have much interest in healing," Idas observed grimly.

Jason quickly explained about the blood and how Asclepius had entrusted it to Chiron.

"After killing the soldiers, the centaurs must have tested the poison on the priests," said Acastus, "just to see what would happen."

They nodded at his words. It had to be just as he said.

Lynceus looked to the northeast, where Mount Ossa reared up above the valley. "So not only are there Zeus-knows-how-many centaurs here," he said at last, "but they've got their hands on something that could wipe out a whole army just like that." He snapped his fingers.

"It's not too late to go back for help, is it?" Admetus wondered aloud.

Clearly his question struck a chord, for the boys all started talking at once.

"How far to Iolcus from here?"

"Could we find the missing horses and ride them?"

"Fool—we could hardly ride those pigs!"

Acastus broke through the babble. "I said all along we should have gone to my father. Then we'd have an army behind us."

Jason didn't dare tell them what Chiron thought, that King Pelias was likely to do as much harm with the Gorgon's blood as the centaurs. Instead he said, "It's too late for arguments or regrets. We're here now and it's all up to us."

"Up to us?" squeaked Lynceus.

"Look what they did to these men," Idas added.

"And we're just boys." Lynceus' voice remained high with fear.

"What are *we* supposed to do?" asked Admetus. "Ask them politely if we can have the jars back?"

Acastus suddenly burst out. "We'll do whatever we have to do. If we get our hands on that poison, we'll give those murderers a taste of their own medicine."

"We *have* to get those jars back to Chiron," said Jason.

Acastus glowered at him. "When the time comes," he answered coldly, "*I'll* decide what to do with the jars. These aren't your people who died here, they're mine."

Jason bristled. He wanted to answer that these were his people, too, but he bit back the words. This was not the time to proclaim his heritage, though he wanted to. Now he had to act like a prince of Iolcus without being one. If only he knew how.

He was deep into this agonizing thought when he saw a slight movement out of the corner of his eye. "Hssst," he whispered to the boys. "There's someone hiding in the bushes over there, by that rock to our right."

Without moving, Acastus let his eyes swivel to the right. "I see it."

Lynceus began to shuffle slowly toward the rock without looking directly at it. Then he made a sudden leap, plunging his hand into the bush. With a triumphant shout, he pulled out his prize by the shoulder.

It was a girl, about twelve years old. Her dark hair was caught up in ribbons behind her ears, and her large brown eyes were wide with fright. She immediately started screaming.

Lynceus stepped back and clamped his hands to his ears. "She's as loud as a harpy!"

"Alcestis!" Acastus exclaimed.

He ran to the girl and grabbed her. At first she tried to push him away, then all at once stopped screaming and threw herself into his arms. "Oh, Acastus, did the gods send you? How I prayed someone would come! How I prayed . . ."

Acastus had to help her to a rock where she could sit down. She bowed her head and, with a mighty effort, stopped sniveling.

"Acastus, who is this?" Jason asked.

"This is Alcestis," Acastus answered. He looked as much embarrassed as surprised. "My sister."

"Your sister?" Jason repeated. "What is *she* doing here?"

"That's what I'd like to know," said Acastus. "She should be back at the palace where she belongs. Not marching around dangerous mountains with soldiers and priests."

At the mention of the soldiers and the priests, everyone grew silent for a moment, thinking about the dead men.

But Alcestis looked up sharply. Her tear-smudged

cheeks blazed bright red. "I belong wherever I want to be," she told her brother. "I suppose you think I should just sit around waiting for Father to marry me off to some cranky old king!"

Jason worked hard at not laughing out loud. Alcestis had certainly gotten over her fears fast enough!

The girl took no notice but continued, "And what about you? Aren't you supposed to be on top of a mountain learning to behave like a prince?"

Admetus stepped forward and offered Alcestis his water skin. "Here," he said. "You look thirsty."

She accepted with a grateful nod. Carefully she removed the stopper and took three measured sips.

"Thank you," she said, handing the water skin back. "At least somebody here has some manners."

"Never mind manners," Acastus interrupted. "Tell us what you're doing here, and be quick about it!"

The girl stared hard at her brother, a small, X-shaped crease appearing between her brows. She sat up straight and adjusted the folds of her rumpled robe. "I came here with the priests, gathering the sacred myrtle from the grove up on the mountain." She spoke in a matter-of-fact voice without looking at any of them, as if she were reciting a tally of provisions.

"Yes, of course," Acastus murmured. "It's almost time for the festival of Dionysus."

"Father—of course—sent those soldiers to guard us," Alcestis continued.

"Of course," Acastus said.

She ignored his interruption. "There was no trouble at all until . . . until the centaurs appeared behind us. I thought they would just pass us by. That's what they've always done before."

"You've done this *before*?" Acastus looked horrified, and Alcestis looked pleased at that.

"I think Captain Lannius suspected something was different, because he ordered the priests to dismount and take me away to safety." Alcestis was well into the story now. "We'd no sooner taken cover than the centaurs attacked the chariots. They panicked the horses, knocked the soldiers to the ground, stamped on them, clubbed them. . . ."

Here her voice began to waver for the first time, and she shut her eyes tight against a bout of tears. "Even Captain Lannius." A single tear ran down her cheek. "They laughed as they killed the men. It happened so fast, brother." Suddenly she shuddered, all her bravado gone.

Admetus put his arm around her, but Alcestis didn't seem to notice. "They smashed the chariots, sent the horses running off. The priests found a hiding place for me and made me stay there when the centaurs came looking for us. In order to keep me safe, they surrendered themselves. They said there were no others. Said they were priests and meant no harm."

"And the centaurs just believed them?" Lynceus asked.

"They would have been too impatient to search any

further," said Jason. "Fighting muddles their wits, just like wine."

"What happened to the priests?" Acastus asked. His questioning, if anything, had become sharper.

Alcestis began to tremble again. This time she wrapped her arms around herself as if to keep warm. "It was so strange, brother. The centaurs had a red jar. They dipped a twig in it and touched the twig to the brow of each of the priests in turn. Then . . . then . . ." Her voice trailed off and her eyes grew moist. She covered her face with her hands.

"It's all right," said Jason, glancing back to where the four corpses lay contorted on the ground. "We can guess what happened after that."

"Why are *you* still here?" Acastus asked. "How could you stand to stay in this ghastly place? Didn't you fear the shades of the murdered men? Or that the centaurs might return?"

Alcestis rubbed away her fresh tears and took a deep breath to steady herself. "I started to look for a way home. I'm not stupid, brother. But I hadn't gone far when I heard the sound of hoofbeats. I ran back to my hiding place and saw another band of centaurs gallop past. There were at least twenty of them. After that even more of them came by, and then more, and I knew I didn't dare move from here."

"How long since the last of them passed?" Jason asked.

"A long while. Hours, I think. I was trying to work up the courage to travel by night if need be. Then I heard you coming. And I hid again."

"But it was *me*, Alcestis," said Acastus. "Why didn't you show yourself at once?"

"Well, how was I to *know* it was you?" She sounded outraged. "I couldn't see your face. I was in hiding. And just look at you! You're filthy and your tunics are torn and you're all dressed like brigands and thieves and . . . and . . . murderers. You were arguing with one another and shouting."

Jason glanced down at his ripped and soiled clothes, at the filth on his legs and arms. The other boys looked as bad. She was right. They *might* have been brigands.

Alcestis touched her brother's hand, too weary to be cross with him anymore. "Can we go home now?" she asked.

"As soon as we finish what we came for," Jason told her, and looked at the others.

They nodded, one after another. They had no other choice.

CHAPTER SEVENTEEN

MOUNT OSSA

It was sharp-eyed Lynceus who led the way. The valley was covered in a shroud of gray, while above them the peak of Mount Ossa stood black against the dull sky. They'd managed to snatch only a few hours of sleep under cover of darkness, knowing that the centaurs would be sleeping as well. But Jason had gotten them moving again well before first light.

Slowly the first red of dawn smeared the horizon. Cold, hungry, tired, they marched on.

"If the centaurs are anywhere, it's here on Mount Ossa," Jason told them. "That's what Chiron said. It's the centaurs' ancient meeting place in times of war. And my guess is that with those jars in their possession, war is what is on their minds."

"I agree," Acastus said. "Finding them quickly has to be our first priority."

"I don't understand why," Alcestis said. "You're far too few to tackle those brutes. Besides, you're just boys. Not men. Not heroes. We should go back to Iolcus and warn Father."

"Not men? We were men enough to get across the mountain and fight off harpies." The look Acastus gave her could have uncurled a pig's tail. "Besides, without chariots, the journey to Iolcus would take days. And we don't have the time."

"Sometimes," Admetus added, "a boy can do what a man cannot."

"Name one thing!" Alcestis put her hands on her hips.

"Quiet!" Jason warned them. "We're on the slopes of Mount Ossa now. The centaurs may have posted look-outs."

Alcestis glanced about. She whispered, "It shouldn't be hard to spot a centaur. They're hardly inconspicuous."

Just then Lynceus made a hissing sound and waved them all into cover. They dropped to their knees and went silent. From the shelter of an acacia bush, they could look far up the slope where a cave mouth gaped open. In front of it stood two centaurs, huge, knobby clubs resting on their shoulders. One of them was yawning.

"There are only two centaurs," Acastus said. "And five of us. Good odds."

"Six," hissed Alcestis.

"No, princess. Leave the fighting to us," Admetus said.

She glared at him, but he stood his ground and did not look away.

"Good odds," Jason told them, "if we can beat them without alerting any of the others. From what Princess Alcestis told us, there must be at least a hundred centaurs gathered here. So far the only advantage we have is that they don't know we're here."

"So what do you suggest?" Idas asked. "That we wait here and ambush them when they come out?"

Jason racked his brains. And then he said, "Suppose . . . suppose there's another way in."

Acastus gave a short, sharp laugh. "If wishful thinking is all you have to offer, why not just *suppose* we have the jars in our hands already."

"A back door of some kind is not that impossible," Jason said, though the more he talked of it, the less sure he was.

"This mountain is probably riddled with cracks and holes," Lynceus said. "One of them could possibly lead into the centaur's cave. But it would take a miracle for us to find it before nightfall."

Alcestis held up her hand. "Then we'll just have to pray for a miracle. Surely the gods, who have taken so much from us already, will grant us one." She said it matter-of-factly, ignoring her brother, who was scornfully shaking his head. Then she clasped her hands and began. "O great Hera, do not desert your children when we need thee most."

All at once Jason was aware of the peacock feather under his tunic. It was growing so hot, he could feel it stinging his flesh. Pulling it out, he held it before him, pinched between his thumb and forefinger. The purple and turquoise colors were aglow.

"Here," he cried, "is our miracle. The answer to Alcestis' prayer."

"A feather?" Acastus sneered. "What can we do with that?"

Alcestis clapped her hands. "Remember, brother, the peacock is sacred to Hera." She turned to Jason. "Where did you find it?"

"Up on the mountains when we were caught in the storm," Jason replied. "I think the goddess must have left it for me."

Acastus smacked Jason's hand, and the peacock feather went flying. A sudden wind set it dancing up the mountainside, away from the cave mouth and the centaur guards. Unaccountably, it hovered in the air, as if waiting for them to follow.

The boys looked stunned. Only Alcestis smiled. Hands on hips, she chided them. "So here we have a group of tired, hungry boys with hardly a decent weapon among them. They know an attack right into the centaurs' cave will never succeed. Perhaps a back way in isn't such a silly idea after all. And maybe—if this feather really is from Hera—we should regard it. After all, what chance do we have of victory if we don't accept the help of the gods?" It was a long speech, and she'd had to take a big gulp of air in the middle of it.

Admetus leaned toward her. "That makes more sense than anything I've heard since we left Chiron's cave. I say we follow the feather."

"And I!" Lynceus whispered.

"And I!" his brother said.

"And I!" Alcestis added.

Only Jason and Acastus were silent, glaring at each other.

Suddenly Jason broke off eye contact and moved forward, keeping low behind more acacia bushes, until he'd caught up with the feather.

The others trailed behind him, all but Acastus. When they'd almost lost sight of him, he suddenly made a dash to catch up.

"What a band of idiots!" he hissed.

"Why did you follow, then?" his sister asked.

"Because I can't fight a hundred centaurs on my own."

Up the mountain they clambered, over rocks and through jagged bushes, the feather bobbing ahead of them.

And then Jason saw something. At first he thought it

was merely a shadow cast on the mountainside or a dark wet spot on the granite face. But when they got a bit closer, he realized it was a narrow cleft in the rock.

"Lynceus, look!" he cried.

Lynceus had already spotted it. "It might just be a niche, going nowhere." But he began to run ahead of Jason.

"Praise the gods!" Alcestis exclaimed triumphantly. "Praise all the gods of Olympus—and especially Hera!"

Jason did not tell her that it was Hera who had wanted her brother and father killed.

They scrambled up to the dark cleft, and Lynceus found a stick, which he pushed into the cleft as far as it would go. It seemed to penetrate straight into the mountain.

Jason looked around for the feather, but it had vanished, seemingly into thin air.

"What do you think, Jason?" Admetus whispered. "Is the opening large enough for us?"

"Maybe."

"Maybe not for Idas." Lynceus elbowed his big brother.

"More importantly—will it get us to the centaurs?" Now Acastus started to take charge.

"There's only one way to find out," Jason answered.

"I wish we had a torch." Lynceus looked around, but they were above the tree line and none of them wanted to go back to look for branches. "Even I can't see in the dark."

"We'll just have to make our way as best we can," Acastus muttered.

"So, do *you* believe now, brother?" Alcestis crowed.

"I'll believe when I see farther into that cleft."

Jason turned sideways and slipped between the rocks, into a fairly wide tunnel. "It's all right," he called back. "We can all fit but—"

Before he finished speaking, Acastus had pressed in behind him, going from morning light to dark in an instant.

"Grab my belt," Jason said. "We'll need to hold on to one another so we don't get separated in the dark."

Acastus grunted, not quite an agreement, then grabbed Jason's belt.

Behind him crowded Admetus, then Alcestis, Idas, and Lynceus, each holding on to the person in front, going down into the awful dark.

CHAPTER EIGHTEEN

THE CAVERN

While the tunnel was wide enough for all of the boys, it was clearly too narrow for any centaur, and too low as well. They had to walk crouching, which was hardest for Idas.

"Most likely," Jason whispered, "the centaurs don't even know about this tunnel." He had stopped for a moment, turning to look back. There wasn't a bit of light.

"Can you still see the entrance?" he called quietly.

"Yes, just barely," came the reply from Lynceus, who was last in line.

Jason moved forward step by cautious step, probing the blackness with his eyes until they ached from the strain. As he moved, he put his hands out and touched cave wall on either side. That, at least, gave him a sense of where he was. The walls were damp and cold, and soon he had to fight shivering.

"I think the tunnel is sloping downward, so take care," he whispered back to Acastus, who shared this with the others.

They crept along for what felt like hours. The dark, the cold, the damp were oppressive. They had no sense of the true passage of time.

"It feels like being buried alive," Admetus whispered.

Maybe, Jason thought, *this* was *a stupid idea. Maybe it's Hera's joke—to bury us all in a rocky grave.*

Suddenly he thought he saw something up ahead. The faintest glint of yellow, a pinpoint of light in the darkness. Jason blinked once, twice. The light was real.

He stopped, turned, whispered to Acastus, "Light. Ahead." Jason could feel the others behind him tense; he heard their sharp intakes of breath. Even more wary now, he proceeded forward. But he'd slipped his sword from its sheath with his right hand, the fingers of his left still brushing along the rough walls. If the centaurs were down there, surely he would hear them.

He slowed even further, knowing they had to be silent as shadows. As he paused, he suddenly made out a distinctive murmur of voices, no louder than a distant trickle of water.

"What's going on?" came Idas' voice. "Why have we stopped?"

"Shhhhh!" Jason cautioned.

They crowded together as much as possible, all listening.

Then Jason started ahead again, Acastus' hand gripping his belt.

The patch of yellow grew larger, the voices became louder. There was enough light now that when Jason looked over his shoulder, he could see the outline of Acastus' face.

"Let go," Jason whispered. "Let my belt go." He pointed to his own eyes, then made a walking movement with his fingers, meaning that he was going for a look.

Acastus nodded and released his hold on the belt.

Then Jason began to creep forward until he could see the end of the tunnel and, ahead, the arching roof of an immense cavern opening out high above him.

The tunnel path suddenly began sloping upward. Dropping to his hands and knees, Jason crawled slowly up the slanting rock. When he reached the edge, he lay flat and peeked over. Below were more centaurs than he'd ever seen in his whole life.

One hundred? Two hundred? he thought. *Maybe even more than that!*

A sea of bearded faces and glossy horses' flanks filled the cavern. Off to the right yawned the mouth of another tunnel, presumably the one that led outside to where the sentries stood.

Pine torches jammed into notches in the wall cast a

flickering yellow light over the whole scene, making shadow centaurs caper along the walls. Resin-scented smoke rose up into Jason's nostrils so that he had to rub his nose vigorously to keep from sneezing.

Acastus slid up beside him and uttered a muted gasp. "There's an army of them!"

It was safe to talk as long as they kept it to a whisper. They would never be heard over the bass hubbub of centaur voices.

"Look over there, on the far side of the cavern," said Jason. He pointed to two jars sitting upon a flat rock with one burly centaur standing guard over them.

Admetus pressed up next to them while the others crouched behind, straining for a view of the cavern.

"Keep down!" Acastus ordered them.

Jason examined the cave before him, assessing it as a hunter checks the lay of the land when tracking his prey. The centaurs had long ago cleared the cave floor of any boulders or large rocks to make room for their gatherings. They had rolled these up against the walls. There seemed to be enough cover there if he chose his moment well and moved stealthily. But Jason knew he would need every bit of skill Chiron had taught him.

Having found somewhere he might hide, he next checked the cleared floor. It was littered with the broken bones of deer, boar, goats, some of them not yet picked clean. Just visible through the milling centaurs was a shallow pit. There were bones in the pit, too, but they were not strewn about. Rather they were carefully reconstructed, forming a complete skeleton of a giant centaur that lay on its side.

Jason felt a prickling at the back of his neck as he realized whose bones those must be.

So, he thought, *that's what has drawn the centaurs here.*

"They're doing something with the jars," Acastus whispered.

Sure enough, one of the centaurs had separated himself from the rest and picked up a jar from the rock.

Jason realized with a start that the centaur was Nessus, with his skull necklace.

"Which jar is he taking?" Acastus asked.

"I'm not sure," Jason replied. "I can't tell the difference in this light. Maybe the healing blood."

"What does he want with that? Nobody here looks sick."

"Let's just watch and see."

Clutching the jar to his chest, Nessus walked toward the pit, and the other centaurs parted before him. An awestruck silence fell over them, and the only sound was the steady clip-clopping of Nessus' feet on the stone floor.

When he reached the pit, Nessus' voice rang out with the force of a gong in the sudden hush. "You all know why we've come here. For too many years we have been divided, quarreling among ourselves instead of uniting. That is why the men of Thessaly have been able to defeat us, to drive us from our lands, to treat us as though we are no better than animals."

The centaurs began an angry murmur that rolled across the cave, echoing from the walls like a wave crashing on a reef.

"But now all that is at an end," Nessus continued, his voice rising above the noise. "Now we shall restore the leader who was lost to us. Through the power of the Gorgon's blood, let him live again!"

Standing on the edge of the pit, he pulled the stopper from the jar and tossed it aside. Then he turned the jar over and poured the contents over the dried-out bones.

For a moment nothing happened, and still the centaurs watched the pit, hardly moving.

The thick blue liquid hissed angrily as it crawled over the bones, sounding like boiling water poured over a cold rock. Haze filled the pit, rising up like morning mist from a lake, only it was shot through with tiny sparks of flame. In the midst of the swirling vapors, a strange movement had begun.

It was difficult to tell from far away—what with the mist and the flames—but gradually the haze lifted, and then the boys and Alcestis could see what the centaurs had already witnessed. A riot of veins, arteries, and sinews had begun wrapping themselves around the bleached skeleton, like ivy running wild over the ruins of an abandoned shrine. Mud-colored flesh sluggishly bubbled over this giant structure, swelling into powerful muscles down the arms and legs. Coarse black hair sprang up along the huge frame, forming thick horsehair in the lower part, curly body hair and beard in the upper.

Then the newly restored body trembled, convulsed. A horse's leg kicked out, a human fist thrust upward. In a series of jerky motions, the gigantic centaur got to his knees, stretched his arms, shook out his shaggy locks, as though shaking off the fog of a long sleep.

As he heaved himself up onto his hooves, all of the other centaurs drew back, gasping in awe. Nessus tossed aside the empty jar, and he, alone, took two steps forward, his arms held up in wonder and in worship.

Slowly the great centaur turned and looked about. He was easily half again as big as Nessus, and beneath his shaggy brows his eyes gleamed like embers. He opened his mouth wide and uttered a long, drawn-out groan.

"Who is that?" Acastus asked. "*What* is that?" There was a tremor in his voice.

Jason's mouth was dry as dust. This was something he had not expected, could hardly explain.

"Kentauros," he said at last, "the ancient leader of the centaurs." He hesitated. "They've brought him back from the dead."

"The *long* dead," Alcestis whispered.

All at once the centaurs began to chant in unison. "KEN-TAU-ROS! KEN-TAU-ROS!"

The name boomed off the cavern walls, redoubling

in volume. Alcestis covered her ears. The boys winced.

Kentauros nodded his head at the ovation, then—almost daintily—trotted out of the pit to stand beside Nessus.

Nessus bowed his head to his king.

"Now we know why they wanted the blood of life," said Lynceus.

The boys and Alcestis started to back away. Jason alone stood his ground. He turned back and said to them, "This is our one chance. While they're distracted, I can go down and get that other jar."

"Not by yourself," said Acastus.

"This is a job for one," Jason insisted.

"Are you so sure you can succeed without me that you'll spurn my help?" Acastus' challenge recalled their previous conversation.

Jason bit his lower lip. He knew there was little time for argument. "All right, but stay low and keep quiet."

"You don't get to give me orders, Goat Boy."

To their left, the ledge sloped downward, ending in a short drop to the cavern floor. There was a boulder there that would keep them hidden. Jason went first, slithering down and jumping the last few feet before diving behind cover. Acastus followed.

The centaurs, all so busy crowding around their new-risen leader, never noticed a thing.

The two boys crouched side by side.

"What now?" Acastus' voice was shaking, though

whether with eagerness or fear Jason couldn't tell.

The chanting was gradually subsiding, but the attention of the centaurs was still entirely focused on Kentauros. In a series of quick sprints, Jason and Acastus dodged from boulder to boulder, stalagmite to stalagmite, hugging the shadows, circling around next to the wall of the great cave.

As the two made their way closer to the remaining jar, Nessus began to speak.

"A new day will soon be dawning outside," he said, "but a greater day is dawning here in this cavern. It is the day of Kentauros!"

A huge cheer went up, and once again the cries of "KEN-TAU-ROS! KEN-TAU-ROS!" filled the air.

Jason darted behind a pile of rocks with Acastus at his heels. Now they were only a short dash from their goal.

"Once we've got the jar—" Jason began, then stopped, shook his head. "I don't know how we're going to get out of here without being spotted."

"We don't need to worry about that," Acastus assured him.

"Why not?"

"Do you think they'll dare come near us when we hold the Gorgon's blood? We could wipe out the whole herd of them with only a sprinkling of it."

Jason swallowed hard. It was a terrible thought. But Acastus was right. "Let's hope it doesn't come to that."

Now Nessus was explaining to Kentauros about the Gorgon's blood and how they had raised him up to lead them in war against the men of Thessaly. The great centaur listened in silence, and then a dreadful thing happened. He laughed. It was a harsh, inhuman sound.

Jason shuddered. *If the dead could laugh*, he thought, *it would sound just like that.*

"The gates of Hades could not hold me!" Kentauros declared, striking a fist against his hairy chest. "How can mortal men stand up to me?" His voice was as terrible as his laugh, cold and hollow as a tomb. He looked squarely at Nessus. "Where is Lapithes, the upstart who slew me?"

Nessus hung his head regretfully. "He is long dead, my king, but his descendants have filled all of Thessaly."

"In that case they will be easy to find—and to kill!" Kentauros cried.

"Easier than you think," Nessus said eagerly. "There are two jars of Gorgon's blood. One of them gave you life, but the other is a poison, a poison so powerful we can use it to destroy all the men of Thessaly."

Again that harsh, inhuman laugh, the sound of vultures at a feast.

Jason and Acastus were now only a couple of yards from their goal. There was still a guard by the flat rock, but with all the excitement he was completely unaware of the two boys behind him.

Without warning, Acastus shouldered Jason aside and made a grab for the red jar.

But he had jumped too quickly. His sandal caught in a crack in the floor, tripping him. He went sprawling, flat on his face, with only the body of the unseeing guard hiding him from the centaurs. All the guard had to do was look round.

"Bring me the blood of death!" Nessus' command rang out.

Desperately Jason made a grab for Acastus' ankle to pull him back, but it was too late.

The guard had started to turn.

CHAPTER NINETEEN

A QUESTION OF DEATH

Up on the ledge the others had been nervously following the progress of the two boys, Alcestis constantly craning forward for a better view.

Admetus was lying on the ledge beside her, with Idas and Lynceus close by.

"Keep back," said Admetus, tugging at her robe. "If you're seen, they'll be on the lookout for others. And then Acastus—"

"None of the centaurs is looking at anything except Kentauros," Alcestis complained, but she slid back.

"I don't blame them," Lynceus muttered. "He's a fearsome-looking brute."

"He's just another centaur," said Idas defiantly.

Now Jason and Acastus were almost within reach of the jar.

"I wish we could do something to help them," Alcestis said.

"The best thing we can do for them is to keep out of sight," Admetus told her.

Just then Acastus made his move and fell. Alcestis and the others stared in horror as the command was issued to bring the jar and the centaur guard began to turn.

"We have to do something," Alcestis gasped. She was leaning forward anxiously, her hands gripping the edge.

"Alcestis, the ledge is giving way!" Admetus warned.

He made a grab for the girl, but it was too late. The outermost part of the ledge—obviously weakened by all the weight upon it—collapsed and sent her tumbling downward. With a startled scream, she hit the stony ground and rolled against the legs of several of the outermost centaurs.

Every one of them—Kentauros included—swung around to face the source of the disturbance. While the guard was distracted, Jason grabbed Acastus by the leg and pulled him back into cover.

"Intruders in the cave!" Nessus bellowed. "The jar—now!"

The guard grabbed the jar and trotted over to his leader, who snatched it away from him.

"If you'd left me alone I might have gotten it!" hissed Acastus.

"Don't be stupid," said Jason. "They're all on their guard now. It's your sister you should be worrying about."

On the ledge above, Idas hauled Admetus and Lynceus back out of sight. "That girl's going to be the death of us," he grumbled.

"No," Admetus retorted, "she's saved Jason and Acastus from getting caught. She's a hero!"

"She's a disaster," Idas said. "And her brother as well."

"Maybe we should get out of here while we still can," Lynceus suggested.

Idas shook his head. "We have comrades down there. We can't abandon them."

Meanwhile, two centaurs had snatched Alcestis up by the arms and brought her to Kentauros, her legs dangling helplessly in the air. She was breathing hard, eyes wide with fear. As she was carried through their midst, the centaurs began to mutter darkly. Kentauros' face was as lean and pale as a skull. He leaned close to her, his voice echoing hollowly through the cavern. "Tell me, child, are you here alone or are there others?"

The question seemed to shake Alcestis out of her horrified stupor, like a cup of cold water dashed across her face. The boys knew all of their lives could depend on what she said now.

Alcestis' mouth opened and closed convulsively, as if she were trying to catch words out of the air. "I'm alone," she said at last in a tiny voice.

"And how did you get past our guards?" Kentauros asked.

"I was . . . here all along." It was hardly more than a breath.

"What was that?" Nessus barked.

Alcestis flinched. "I was here all along," she repeated, more loudly this time.

Nessus' eyes darted around suspiciously. "Doing what? Spying?"

"I was gathering flowers outside." Alcestis' voice was steadier now, the words coming more easily. "I saw centaurs coming up the hill, so I ran in here. I was afraid. I've been warned against centaurs."

"You've been here unseen all this time?" Nessus seemed skeptical.

Alcestis nodded.

The centaurs let out a rumble of displeasure and one bellowed, "Torture her!"

"That'll make her speak the truth!" shouted another.

Alcestis' face was pale in the torchlight, but she did not weep. If anything, the calls of the centaurs gave her strength.

On the ledge, Admetus was clawing at the stone beneath him in helpless frustration. "You were wrong about her, Idas," he whispered as the centaurs' threats boomed louder and louder. "She's braver than any of us."

"You may be right," Idas agreed. "But I doubt her

courage will save her now."

Suddenly Kentauros let out a contemptuous roar that silenced his followers. "Has centaur blood grown thinner since my day? Is one human child enough to throw you into a panic?"

He gazed around at his fellow centaurs, and one by one by one they hung their heads in shame. Even Nessus looked away, grinding his teeth in humiliation.

"Give her to me," Kentauros ordered, his voice a clap of thunder.

He gripped Alcestis around the waist with both hands and lifted her up so that she was staring him in the face, the tips of their noses only inches apart. The girl shook uncontrollably.

"I'm curious about this potion of yours," Kentauros said to Nessus. "Let me see what it does."

Obediently Nessus removed the stopper from the jar.

"You see this jar, girl?" Kentauros asked.

Alcestis' eyes flickered to where Nessus was standing.

"Would you like a drink of what's inside it?"

Alcestis pursed her lips tightly and shook her head.

"Why not?" Kentauros' lips curled back in a malevolent grin. "You must be thirsty after hiding for so long."

Still there was no reply.

"Go on," Kentauros coaxed, "just a sip."

Alcestis answered in a near whisper, but her words could be heard all over the cavern. "Drink it yourself."

Kentauros' grin twisted into a snarl. "The race of man!" he sneered. "What have we to fear from them? Just see how easily they break!"

So saying, he lifted Alcestis up above his head and hurled her away from him. She flew across the cavern and hit the rock wall with a sickening thud. She flopped limply to the cave floor and lay there, unmoving.

Trembling, Acastus reached for his sword. Before he could make another move, Jason clamped a hand over his mouth and wrestled him to the ground.

"No, not now!" he rasped urgently into the prince's ear. "You'll get us all killed, and who'll stop Kentauros then?"

"Ken-tau-ros! Ken-tau-ros!" Slowly the chant was starting up again. "KEN-TAU-ROS! KEN-TAU-ROS!"

Kentauros spread his arms wide, accepting the adulation of his followers.

Nessus carefully replaced the stopper in the jar and waited for the uproar to die down. "You will all see the effects of the Gorgon's blood soon enough," he told Kentauros, "when we use it to destroy the men of Iolcus at a stroke. If any are left, we will slaughter them ourselves. And when Iolcus has fallen, all of Thessaly will tremble before us!"

A ghastly cheer shook the walls of the cavern.

Acastus' breast was heaving with anger, and his face had turned bright red. Jason knew it wasn't safe to release him yet. "Think of your city," he urged. "We can't afford to let ourselves be captured now."

Finally Acastus seemed to pull himself together, and Jason slowly loosened his hold.

"They will pay for this," Acastus vowed in a hoarse whisper.

"They will pay mightily," Jason agreed.

"I have spent long enough in this tomb," Kentauros bellowed. "I want to see the sky, the mountains, the plains of Thessaly."

"Lead us, then," Nessus encouraged him, "and we will follow."

The ranks parted before him, and Kentauros trotted into the tunnel and out of sight. The other centaurs charged after him like a vast river pouring through a canyon. The clatter of their hooves echoed deafeningly, then faded away.

The boys were alone in the vast, empty silence of the cavern. The centaurs had taken the red jar with them.

Acastus jumped up at once and ran to Alcestis. Dropping to one knee, he took her by the wrist.

Jason stood by him, his hand hovering uncertainly over the prince's shoulder. He wasn't sure if a gesture of comfort would be welcome.

The other three boys came hurrying down from the ledge.

"Acastus, what can we do?" Idas asked.

Acastus' head was bowed low. "Nothing," he said with a groan. "Alcestis is dead."

There was a long, miserable silence, then Admetus spoke up.

"You're wrong, Acastus. There is something we can do."

The others all turned to face him. Cradled in his arm was the discarded jar that had held the blood of life.

"It's not completely empty," he said.

CHAPTER TWENTY

A MATTER OF LIFE

They gathered around Admetus, and Lynceus peered into the jar. He wrinkled his nose. "There can't be more than a couple of drops in there."

"What use can it be?" Idas asked. "They needed the whole jar to raise up Kentauros."

"Yes, but he'd been dead for centuries," Admetus reminded them. "Alcestis is newly dead. This might be enough."

Lynceus squinted at Jason. "What do you think, Jason?"

Jason's throat tightened. He didn't like the thought of using the Gorgon's blood, not after all that Chiron had told him. The gods could punish them all for such a thing. "It . . . might work." He hesitated. "But do we have the right?"

"The right?" Admetus cried. "The right to *heal*? The right to save a life?"

"She's not sick," said Idas. "She's dead."

Jason nodded. "We're not talking about *saving* a life, Admetus. There's no life there to save. We're talking about bringing Alcestis back from the grave."

"She's not *in* her grave," Admetus cried. "She's not even cold yet."

"We aren't gods," Jason said. "They don't like humans to take on their roles."

"We're not even the sons of gods like the healer Asclepius was," said Lynceus

"When you're dead, you're dead, and that's that," Idas declared sullenly.

For a long while no one spoke. It was as if they were waiting for another voice—perhaps Chiron's—to intervene and tell them what to do.

At last Jason said, "What do *you* say, Acastus? She's your sister, after all."

Acastus had been unusually silent. He looked pale and drawn as he spoke. "What should I do? If my father knew that Alcestis was killed, and I could have brought her back, and didn't . . ." He took a deep breath, a gulp that was almost a sob. "But Alcestis was devoted to the gods. Perhaps she wouldn't want to defy their will." He stared down at his dead sister as if asking her advice.

“Suppose, Acastus, suppose the gods *want* her to live,” Admetus pleaded, holding the jar before him. “Suppose that’s why they’ve left us these last few drops of healing blood.”

“Maybe we’re supposed to save the blood for another time,” Lynceus said.

Acastus stood up slowly, carefully, his sister in his arms. “It’s true she was no warrior.” He was looking directly at Jason as he spoke, but he was addressing all of them. “But if not for her, Jason, it would be you and me lying there dead. It would be all of us. We owe our lives to her.”

“I know that,” said Jason. “But Chiron sent us to retrieve the Gorgon’s blood, not use it.”

“How does that matter now?” asked Admetus. “Both jars have already been used. There’s not enough left here to be worth taking back.”

“Maybe not,” Jason said, “but there’s something else we have to remember. Something Chiron told me. Asclepius raised the dead with the Gorgon’s blood, and Zeus destroyed him for it.”

Idas rubbed his chin ruefully. “We’ll have a hard enough time stopping the centaurs without bringing the anger of Zeus down on our heads.”

“I didn’t see Nessus catch a thunderbolt when he raised Kentauros,” said Lynceus.

“The gods can keep a grudge for a long, long time,” said Jason, thinking of Hera and her hatred for Pelias.

"We don't know what might happen or when."

"We never know that anyway," said Lynceus with a shrug.

"Only one of us need take the chance," said Acastus, "and it should be me. After all, I'm her brother."

The boys all nodded at that.

Jason looked at them steadily. "Are we agreed, then, that we're going to do it?"

"As long as we have that blood with us, we're always going to be tempted to use it," said Lynceus. "We may as well get it over with."

"Idas?"

Idas nodded slowly. "I suppose in the end death is the one enemy we all face. Let's see if we can beat him, just this once."

"Admetus?"

Admetus answered by holding out the jar.

"All right, then," said Jason, relieved that they'd come to a decision. He didn't think Chiron would disapprove.

Acastus reached a hand out for the jar, but Admetus clutched it to his chest. "Not this time, Acastus. This time you'll give way to me. I was beside her when she fell. If I had been quicker, I could have caught her. But I didn't. I failed, just as I always fail back home in Pherae. Why else do you think my father sent me to Chiron to be trained?"

"It should be my responsibility," said Acastus. "Are you forgetting the risk?"

"Yes," Jason agreed. "The gods—"

"If saving a brave and precious life offends the gods," Admetus said firmly, "then they can take out their anger on me."

Now, for the first time, Jason could see that Admetus was truly a prince and a hero. It had little to do with where or to whom he had been born. It had to do with taking responsibility.

Even Acastus seemed to have a new respect for his cousin. He set his sister's body back down on the ground and stepped aside for Admetus, who crouched by her and gently tipped over the jar.

A bead of blue liquid took shape on the rim and fell onto the girl's brow. A second, smaller drop formed and fell onto the first, merging into a single stain. A third drop fell onto her lips, tinting them.

The jar was dry now, so Admetus set it aside and stood up and, with the other boys, waited for something to happen. It was so quiet in the cave, Jason could have sworn they had all stopped breathing.

The effect was not so dramatic as it had been with Kentauros, yet the boys were amazed to see the blue stain on Alcestis' brow and lips gradually disappear, like rainwater soaking into parched ground.

Then the moments dragged by slowly with no sign of any further change.

"It didn't work," Lynceus cried. "There wasn't enough of it."

"No," Admetus said, pointing. "Look!"

A tremor had begun to run through Alcestis' body. Her chest moved up and down as she sucked new breath into her lungs. The fingers of her right hand twitched as though grasping air.

"By Ares' chariot!" Idas exclaimed.

Alcestis was blinking now, and she moved a languid hand before her eyes to keep out the light of the torches.

"Sister . . ." Acastus bent over and helped her sit, then stand. For a moment she looked at each of them in turn slowly, as if she could not quite remember who they were. Or where she was.

When she spoke, her voice was small and distant. "I thought I was somewhere else. . . ." She shook her head. "No, I can't remember. The last thing I saw was the centaur. Kentauros. Big, ugly face. Nose the size of a pitcher. Was it a dream?"

Her eyes grew wide with fright, and Acastus put a reassuring arm around her trembling shoulders.

"Not a dream, then. He threw me and . . . what happened then?"

"You were stunned," Jason answered, before anyone could utter the truth. "You were stunned. Out cold. You're fine now."

That last, at least, was true, he reflected. She had not so much as a single visible bruise on her body, yet she'd been smashed against the stone by Kentauros' terrible strength.

All the boys exchanged glances, silently agreeing that they would never reveal to Alcestis what had really happened.

"Yes, I feel fine," Alcestis said, running her hands down her robe to straighten it. She looked around the cavern, baffled. "Where did they all go?"

"They left you for . . . dead," said Acastus. "They've gone on to Iolcus."

"Well, why are we just standing here?" Alcestis demanded, shaking off his arm. "Shouldn't we go after them?"

"Yes, we should," said Jason. "But how on earth are we going to catch them?"

Now that they were no longer concerned with Alcestis' fate, the same awful question occurred to all of them.

"If we had chariots," Acastus said, "we'd have a slim chance at least. But it's miles and miles to the nearest town."

Alcestis placed her hands on her hips and raised a sardonic eyebrow at her brother. "Acastus, have you lost your wits? Of course there's a way. The river road."

CHAPTER TWENTY-ONE

THE CHALLENGE

They had to trek westward for two hours to reach the river. When they came over the grassy rise and saw it spread out in the sun below them, Alcestis pointed it out proudly, as if it were a tapestry she'd sewn with her own hands. "You see, that will be much faster than going on foot."

"Probably faster than a chariot, too," said Jason. "A river doesn't tire the way a horse does."

"Where does this river go?" asked Lynceus.

"All the way to Lake Boebis," replied Alcestis.

"And the southernmost shore of the lake is only a few miles from Iolcus," said Acastus.

"That's all very well," said Idas, his hand shading his

eyes as he scanned the river, "but are we going to swim all the way?"

"There should be a ferry around here somewhere," Alcestis said.

"Yes, there it is," said Lynceus, pointing upstream where the river bowed toward the east. A flat-bottomed raft had been dragged up on shore and anchored to a birch tree.

They raced down the incline. Near the raft was a small stone-built cottage with a ferryman sitting on a tree stump and carving something out of a stick of wood. From time to time he paused to pluck a blueberry from a pouch at his side and pop it into his mouth.

"Hoi!" Jason called out, and the ferryman looked up to register the approach of the newcomers, then went back to his work. He was a muscular, barrel-chested fellow with short-cropped sandy hair and a grizzled beard.

"We'd like to hire your ferry," Acastus called as they drew closer.

The ferryman looked up and spat out a blueberry stem. "Of course you would. Why else would you be here? Just let me finish carving this peg and I'll take you over."

"We don't want to go across the river," said Acastus. "We want to go down it, to Lake Boebis."

"No, I don't do that," said the ferryman, forcing his

knife through a knot in the wood. "Back and forth, that's what I do, one side to the other."

"Look, we have to get to the city of Iolcus as fast as we can," said Admetus. "It's very important."

"Then I'd start walking if I were you," the ferryman said without looking up. "It's a long way."

Alcestis nudged Acastus. "Tell him!" she whispered. "Tell him why we must get there quickly."

"No," said Jason. "It has to stay a secret."

Acastus nodded his agreement, then walked up to the ferryman. "I am Acastus," he announced, "Prince of Iolcus, son of King Pelias."

The ferryman paused to pick another stem out of his teeth. "I am Argos, son of Arestor," he said, "and I doubt if you've heard of me either."

The side of Acastus' mouth twitched irritably. He fingered his amulet. "Look, man, this is solid gold, and those red stones are rubies. I'll give it to you in exchange for the ferry. It's worth far more than your boat."

"To you it may be, but that boat's my livelihood. I can't make a living out of a bit of metal, no matter how pretty and shiny it is."

"We'll bring it back, I swear," Jason assured him.

"Bring it back?" Argos raised a skeptical eyebrow. "I doubt that. From the looks of you, not one of you knows how to steer a craft through rough waters. No, I think it best if you just go on your way and leave me to my business."

Idas had already lost patience. "We'll fight for it, if need be," he declared, smacking his fist into the palm of his hand.

The ferryman considered this a moment. "All right, then," he said, rising to his feet. "I'll wrestle each of you in turn, one throw to decide each contest. If any one of you can beat me, I'll accept the prince's trinket and let you have what you need. If I am unbeaten, then you must still give me the amulet and go away."

Standing up, he was a good head taller than Idas, and a lot wider, too.

"So either way I lose my amulet," Acastus muttered.

Argos shrugged. "If you don't like the bargain—"

"No—we accept," Jason said quickly. He turned and added to Acastus, "We don't have any other choice."

Acastus growled. "But it's my amulet."

"Shut up!" Idas, Lynceus, and Admetus said together.

Jason pulled the boys aside. "Look—one of us alone is no match for him, but—"

"But there are five of us," Admetus pointed out. "He's bound to tire."

Idas was already stripping off his belt and his pack. Acastus tugged his arm to keep him back. "You hold off till last, Idas. You're our best chance, but only if you let the others wear him down first."

Idas gritted his teeth ruefully. "I don't like to stand and watch, but it's a good tactic," he conceded.

"Go ahead, Admetus," Acastus urged his cousin.

"You can have the first chance to prove yourself."

Admetus did not look confident, but dropping his weapons, he stepped forward bravely. As he approached the ferryman, he fell into a crouch, moving warily from side to side. Argos still had his arms folded, and his eyes followed his youthful opponent as if he were watching an insect scuttling across the ground in front of him.

Finally Admetus mustered his courage and charged. He wrapped his arms around Argos' waist and tried to lift him. He might have been trying to uproot an oak tree for all the success he had. The ferryman let him grunt and heave for a while. Then he hooked an arm around the boy, yanked him effortlessly off his feet, and tossed him aside.

Admetus thudded to the ground, rolled over three times, and lay there groaning. Alcestis hurried to his side and helped him up.

"You're next, Lynceus," Acastus said.

"It's an honor, of course," said Lynceus, "but I would like to offer someone else the opportunity to—"

"Go on!" Idas barked at him.

Lynceus made a feeble attempt at a grin. Carefully setting aside his pack and his sword, he advanced briskly. He feinted to the right and left in a series of quick movements, then instantly retreated. The ferryman did not react.

Lynceus began to circle the grizzled ferryman, making jabbing motions with his arms. Gradually he drew closer and closer until he strayed within Argos' reach.

The ferryman immediately seized him by the arm and flung him over his shoulder like an empty grain sack. Lynceus tumbled head over heels, then slowly got to his feet, clutching his shoulder and grimacing.

The sight of his brother's pain was all the prompting Idas needed. "To Hades with your plan, Acastus!" he cried out, and charged the ferryman with unexpected speed, ramming his shoulder into the man's midriff. Argos staggered back, winded. Idas grabbed his leg with both hands and tried to flip him over, but the ferryman planted himself like a rock and clamped his arms around Idas' waist. Flipping the boy completely upside down, he flung Idas onto his back.

As soon as he landed, Idas leaped up and kicked the ground in frustration. He made to attack again, but Argos raised a cautionary hand.

"The rules were one throw wins," he said. "Don't turn your courage to dishonor, young warrior."

Idas simmered for a moment, then turned and stalked away.

"This isn't going to work, is it?" Jason said softly to Acastus.

"Do you have a better plan?" Acastus snapped back.

"Not yet," Jason admitted.

"Then you can stand here and watch while I fight. At least I have the courage to try."

He stripped down for the contest and advanced toward the ferryman. Falling into a fighting crouch, he stretched his arms out in front of him, searching for a hold.

"Go on, Acastus!" Idas roared. "Knock him senseless!"

The others joined in the cheering, all except Jason. If Acastus lost, it would all be up to him, and he knew he could not outwrestle Argos. The ferryman's muscles had grown massive from poling his boat back and forth across the river; he was probably strong enough to toss a bull on its head.

No, Jason thought, *Chiron's always said my wits were my best weapon.*

Suddenly he was shaken from his thoughts by a huge groan from his companions. Argos had thrown Acastus flat on his back. Winded, the prince clambered painfully to his feet, spurning the help that was offered to him.

Jason realized the ferryman was gazing directly at him.

"There's only you left now, youngster," he said. "Do you want to take a beating, too, or will you just concede?"

Jason looked around at the others, their faces expectant, but not hopeful. Then he looked at the wide expanse of the river. All at once he knew what he had to do.

"My friends are all better fighters than I," he said humbly. "What would it prove for you to flatten me as well?"

"In that case," said the ferryman, folding his arms, "the contest is over."

CHAPTER TWENTY-TWO

THE FERRYMAN'S PRICE

Even Acastus was stunned. "I never really thought you were a coward, Jason. Not until now."

"Jason, fight him!" Idas roared. "Show some honor!"

Jason waved them to silence and addressed the ferryman. "The contest isn't over, not if you give me the chance to best you in some other way."

Argos eyed him suspiciously. "What do you mean?"

"There are better tests of strength than wrestling."

"Oh, are there? And what might those be?"

Jason shrugged and pointed to the river. "Could you hit the far bank with a stone?"

The ferryman looked across the water and stroked his grizzled beard. "No man could throw that far."

"Let that be our contest, then," said Jason. "Whoever can hit the far side with a stone wins."

"It's a waste of time," said Argos. "Let's just wrestle and get it over with."

"Don't tell me you're not up to the challenge!" Jason exclaimed.

For a moment the ferryman bristled. Then he gave a chuckle. "You've nerve enough," he said. "I suppose you're a prince, too."

"No," said Jason, "I'm Jason of Mount Pelion. I'm a student of the centaur Chiron."

"Now him I've heard of," said Argos. "They say the pines on that mountain of his make the finest ships' timbers in all of Thessaly."

"So do you agree to *my* challenge?" Jason asked.

Argos stroked his beard a few times, then agreed. He looked around the bank and picked up a stone the size of his fist. He hefted it in his hand to test its weight and nodded. "This should suit. Now you pick one."

Jason scanned the ground at his feet and picked out a much smaller stone, one he could completely enfold in his fingers.

"Right, then," said the ferryman, "would you care to go first, Jason of Mount Pelion?"

"No, it's your boat and your river. You take the first throw."

Argos shook his arm to loosen up the muscles, then he drew it back. With a grunt he launched his rock into the air. All eyes followed it as it arced over the river. Only a few feet short of the far bank, it dropped into the water with a splash. Argos turned to Jason and grinned. "Give up?"

Idas shook his head gloomily. "You'll never match that, Jason."

For a moment, Jason acted as if awed by the ferryman's strength. His jaw dropped. He took a deep breath.

Acastus gave Jason a contemptuous glare. "What did you think you were doing? You can't beat him any more than we could."

Jason turned to Lynceus. "Loan me your sling, would you?"

Lynceus pulled the sling from his belt and handed it over. "You might as well have it," he said, wincing. "That brute bashed in my shoulder when we wrestled, so I can't use it anyway."

The ferryman folded his arms and looked from Jason to the far bank of the river, then back again. He said nothing, but his eyes had narrowed warily.

Jason placed the stone in the sling and started to wind his arm. He swung the sling around, twirling it faster and faster until his arm started to ache. Then he let loose the missile. The stone shot over the water faster than a racing bird. Then it struck the edge of the sand on the other side.

Admetus and Lynceus cheered uproariously.

Acastus and Idas looked to the ferryman, uncertain of how he would react.

It was Alcestis, though, who said what the others were thinking. Frowning at Jason, she shook her head. "That was hardly fair. You were supposed to throw the stone."

"No," said Jason, "the challenge was to hit the far bank with a stone. I never said anything about throwing."

All at once Argos' grim face broke into a wide grin, and he laughed uproariously. "He used his head," he said, tapping himself on the temple. "That's more than any of the rest of you bothered to do."

Jason tried to hand the sling back, but Lynceus declined it. "Keep it, Jason. It's a poor enough gift, but it's no use to me with my shoulder wrenched like this. And take my pouch of stones as well. You've more than earned them."

"We can have the boat, then?" Acastus asked.

Argos thrust out his hand. "The agreement was that I would sell it to you if any of you could best me."

Acastus reluctantly slipped off his amulet and dropped it into the ferryman's palm. Argos stuffed it carelessly into his belt.

"Time's running out," said Jason. "We've got to get started."

"I should warn you," said Argos, wrinkling his nose, "I've seen a goat swim faster than this raft. She'll be dashed to pieces before she gets in sight of Lake Boebis."

"Hoi!" exclaimed Jason. "You said you built her with your own hands."

"Yes, to carry passengers, baggage, even goats and sheep, from one side of the river to the other. I didn't build her to go through the Dragon's Mouth."

"What's that?" The boys spoke as one.

Shaking his head over their ignorance, Argos told them. "A narrow canyon some miles downriver where the water runs fast as the wind. The rocks are like giant fangs. They'd chew up my poor ferry and spit her out as driftwood."

"Then you've cheated us!" Acastus cried.

The old ferryman shook his finger at Acastus. "If you're to be a king, my boy, you should be slower to judge people."

They all stared at him, confused and angry.

"I said I'd sell you what you need," the ferryman told them. "I've another boat that can do the journey. Oh, yes, she'll get you where you want to go, if you speak sweetly to her."

He turned and walked away, beckoning them to follow. Beyond the cottage was a small inlet where a sheet of canvas had been thrown over some large object that lay close to the water's edge. Argos gripped the edge of the sheet and yanked it away.

Jason gasped and Lynceus let out a low whistle. Even Acastus looked impressed.

"She's a beauty," said Admetus.

Argos nodded. "I think Athena herself must have guided my hand in fashioning her."

Jason was inclined to agree. On trips with Chiron, he'd seen clumsy fishing boats casting their nets in the sea, always within safe reach of the shore. But this boat was as different from one of them as a hawk is from a hen.

Where the ferry was wide and flat, this vessel was as sharp and sleek as a needle and twenty feet long. A pair of bright green eyes was painted on the bow, while stripes of blue and green, shaped like feathers, swept down both sides.

Alcestis walked up to the boat and ran her hand down the painted feathers. "She looks like a bird, not a boat."

Argos nodded again. "I call her the *Swift*. I built her with my son, and for him." There was a sudden sadness in his voice. "We were going to transport her north to the great River Peneus and journey down the river, through the Vale of Tempe to the sea. What adventures we might have had then! I was even going to fit her with a sail like the great ships of Egypt and Crete, but . . ." His voice trailed off, and his eyes seemed suddenly rheumy with tears.

"What happened?" Alcestis asked.

Argos grew even more solemn. "A few months ago my boy was climbing among the cliffs, searching for eagles' eggs, when he lost his grip and fell to his death. He made his voyage—not with me, but with Charon, the ferryman of the Underworld, over the cursed River Styx."

"I'm sorry," she said, and put a hand on his arm. "He must have been very proud of this boat."

Argos patted her hand, then looked away at the hill they had run down. "I buried him up there, overlooking this very spot where we labored so hard. I left him with provisions for his journey and a bronze token in his mouth to pay for his passage across the Styx."

Acastus cleared his throat and looked abashed. "It's worth more than a gold amulet," he said. "More than anyone could ever pay you for it."

"I wouldn't entrust her to you if there weren't one of you worthy of that trust," said Argos, laying his broad hand on Jason's shoulder. "Now, if you're in as big a hurry as you say, we'd best get her into the water."

"First a prayer for the journey," Alcestis said. And though her brother raised his eyebrows, he didn't argue the point.

"Wait!" Argos cried. He ran back to his little cottage and returned with a jug of fresh water and a basket of bread, olives, and salted fish. "For the journey."

Alcestis spilled a bit of the water on the side of the boat and into the river, saying, "God of the river, son and cousin of great Poseidon, smooth the water for us and carry us over the broad waves safely to the sweet shores of Lake Boebis."

While the others manhandled the boat off the bank and into the shallows, Argos drew Jason aside.

"Not an easy crew to manage, are they?"

"No, they're not," Jason agreed, "but it was worse only a few days ago. And to tell you the truth, I've never been in a boat before."

"You're captain enough for the journey," said the ferryman. "After all, you can only go one way—downriver. Just keep an eye out for the unanticipated. And remember, always expect more of yourself than you do of your crew, and the rest will follow."

Jason smiled. "Chiron said something like that, too."

"Then he must be wise, for a centaur." Argos slipped the gold amulet out of his belt and offered it to Jason. "Here, take this. It's no use to me. You can give it back to your friend Acastus, if you like."

Jason looked to where the others were all sliding the boat into the river. Lynceus tripped and plunged into the water. There was a chorus of good-natured laughter, and Acastus took Lynceus' arm to help him up.

"No, you keep it," said Jason. "He's better off without it. And I think he may be starting to understand that himself."

CHAPTER TWENTY-THREE

THE DRAGON'S MOUTH

Soon all six of the travelers were seated in the boat, alongside the jug of fresh water and basket of bread, olives, and salted fish. Then the ferryman waded into the river and gave the *Swift* a hefty shove to help it out of the shallows.

"Remember, Argos, son of Arestor, is my name," the ferryman called after them, his arm held up in a salute. "If you ever need a swift ship built, you know who to send for."

"I'll remember," Jason called back. "Perhaps one day we'll make a voyage worthy of your son's memory."

The boat had been equipped with two pairs of oars, one each for Argos and his son. Now Jason, Acastus, Idas, and Admetus were squeezed side by side onto the two benches with an oar each to handle. Lynceus was seated at the back, where he could watch the course ahead and cry out corrections to the rowers. Occasionally he thumped out a beat for them with the flat of his hand.

Alcestis leaned over the front of the boat like a figurehead, trailing her fingers in the water. "I'll keep my eyes peeled for river nymphs," she said.

"Better yet, look out for rocks," her brother told her.

At first Jason found the sensation of water beneath him unsettling; he half expected the boat to sink suddenly, leaving them all to flounder in the swift-flowing river. But soon his unease gave way to a sense of freedom, and he felt as if he'd been born to be on a boat.

Once the rowers had settled into their rhythm, the sweep of the oars and the force of the current drove the craft forward like a bird, skimming over the surface of the water. With the sun shining overhead and the fresh breeze in their faces, they all felt their strength renewed.

"The centaurs will have to go the long way around the lake," said Acastus, "while we can go directly across. We might even overtake them, if we're lucky."

"Yes, *if* we're lucky," Jason agreed. For the first time in days he felt a small measure of hope in his heart.

They rowed for hours until they all felt as if their arms would drop off. Pausing only briefly for a few mouthfuls of bread and olives and fish, and a gulp of water, they rowed steadily on.

By now the river was growing narrower and faster. So wide and relatively placid back at Argos' ferry, it had become a seething torrent, bubbling and frothing under the keel of the speeding boat. They rowed now not to propel the boat forward but to stop it from hitting rocks or diving down huge, cascading riffles. They were all wet from spray, and when the sun dropped behind occasional clouds, the air grew cool, even chilling. Alcestis was trembling with cold, as was Lynceus, but the rowers perspired from their efforts.

Along the shoreline, the grass gave way to moss-covered crags that reared up on either side like the ill-tended walls of an abandoned city. The rushing water in that stony valley sounded like a long hoarse breath.

"We could pull ashore here," Lynceus said, "and make the rest of the journey on foot."

"And find Iolcus a dead city?" said Acastus. "Never! We go on to the lake."

Now they fell under the shadow of the cliffs, and the air grew suddenly darker and colder.

"I hope we've made the right choice," Admetus worried. "None of us are sailors."

"Argos said the boat could make it," said Jason.

Lynceus sighed. "You're putting a lot of confidence in him. He's only a ferryman."

"I think he's a lot more than that," Jason said.

"Rock dead ahead!" Alcestis shrieked, pulling herself back from the front of the boat.

Lynceus half stood, then sat down abruptly, screaming, "Pull left! Hard left!" He signaled with his hand and shouted again, "Left!"

The rowers dug their oars into the water and tried to drag the *Swift* from her course, but it was too late. The prow glanced off the rock, and the boat jerked aside as if she had been punched in the jaw. She spun around in the churning water, then righted herself and slipped back into the center.

"What's happening?" Alcestis called out in a quavering voice. "Are we sinking?"

Jason leaned over, quickly examining the hull. "No, there's no damage," he assured her. "Argos built her to handle rough waters."

Now they used the oars only to fend off the approaching rocks.

Suddenly Jason felt a chill mist at his back, like a puff of icy breath. Glancing over his shoulder, he saw a cloud of spray filling the canyon ahead.

"Listen to that noise!" Acastus cried.

The rush of the water was getting louder, booming off the canyon walls. Lynceus was peering through the mist, straining his eyes to the utmost.

"Hang on tight," he warned. "All that spray can only mean one thing."

"Waterfall," Jason said under his breath.

"What?" Admetus, his seat partner, strained to hear.

"Waterfall!" Jason shouted.

The sound of crashing water was almost deafening now, and the little boat was completely engulfed in spray.

"Hang on!" Lynceus cried again.

Alcestis began uttering a steady stream of prayers, calling on Zeus, Hera, Poseidon, and every other god she could think of to protect them. A gut-jarring lurch cut her off as the boat launched into the air.

For a few breathless seconds the *Swift* really was flying: down, down, down the side of the falls. The boys and Alcestis had to hold on to the sides of the boat in order not to be thrown into the roiling river.

Then the *Swift* hit the water again with a sickening smack that pitched her little crew flat on their faces. The boat spun helplessly in powerful eddies as one by one the boys scrambled back to their places, grabbing at the oars that threatened to slide out of their locks. Alcestis alone remained where she'd been thrown.

"Grab your oars and try to steady her!" Jason yelled above the noise of the river, and the boys were quick to do his bidding.

They stabbed the oars into the water, using them to resist the whirling currents. Gradually they gained control of the *Swift* and managed to aim her prow directly downstream once more.

"To the right!" Lynceus yelled.

Ahead of them, a round boulder rose out of the water like the humped back of a giant serpent. The rowers tried to turn the boat, but the rapids had them completely in their grip. Idas tried to fend the boulder off with his oar, but the impact knocked the oar out of his grasp.

"Look out!" he yelled, leaning into the water and retrieving the oar.

Now the driving current slammed them against the rock, and they were jolted to the right. The boat shivered and bounced on the water.

"It's all right!" Lynceus exclaimed with a nervous laugh. "We're still afloat."

"Hold on to your oars!" Acastus ordered. "There are plenty more rocks ahead!"

The *Swift* swerved and tilted, the prow rising suddenly upward, then dipping sharply away.

"More spray ahead!" Lynceus warned.

They held tightly to their oars. This time Alcestis was not alone in her prayers.

The next waterfall was bigger and higher. The rushing torrent threw the *Swift* into the empty air. Screams erupted all around. Idas, forgetting his prayers, hurled a bitter curse at the gods for their indifference.

This time when they came down, it was with a smack that threw them to the floor of the boat in a tangle of limbs. A huge plume of water erupted from the stern and crashed down on them.

"We're going to sink!" Admetus cried.

"There's a jug here somewhere." On his stomach still, Lynceus scrambled about, looking for the jug.

"I've got it!" Alcestis called, and immediately started bailing by scooping up water and flinging it over the side.

Jason pulled himself onto his knees. Gazing in horror through the spray, he saw that they were headed straight for a rock as sharp as the beak of a monstrous bird. Clearly it would stab right through the hull and smash the boat to splinters. Leaping to his feet, he seized his oar and lunged, driving the oar at the rock. The wood snapped in two under the impact, and Jason was thrown off his feet. His arms flapped uselessly, and he toppled over the side into the churning water.

Lost in the chaotic flood, he kicked upward with all his might. His head broke the surface and he coughed, spitting out water. The eddies twisted him giddily about; the river spun around him in a blur of silver-and-white foam.

Then he saw the keel of the *Swift* veering sharply toward him. He tried to grab a breath and dive under it, but too late. The edge of the wood smacked him in the head. Pain lanced his skull. Blackness closed over him, and he was sucked down into the hungry waters.

CHAPTER TWENTY-FOUR

THE LAKE

Is this what it's like to be dead?

The thought seemed to come to Jason from nowhere, and that was exactly where he was—nowhere.

All around him was a darkness so complete, it was as if he were in a bottomless pit of tar. He could feel nothing of his own body: not an arm or leg.

Is this is how the spirits of the dead are supposed to be, he thought, *like a thin, drifting shadow?* Chiron had taught him that spirits could be summoned back briefly to the upper world by a sacrifice of blood to speak their secrets to the living. *Will anyone ever bother to summon me back, or does my story die with me?*

Then, suddenly, he saw a glimmer of light, heard the slap of water on a nearby shore.

Now he knew exactly where he was. The light was the lantern of Charon, the ferryman of the Underworld, who was waiting to carry him across the River Styx to the Land of the Dead. The sound he was hearing was the murmur of that poisoned river.

"Jason?"

That voice. How strange that the ferryman of the dead should address him in a young girl's voice.

"What's happening? Is he waking up?"

That voice sounded familiar, too. Lynceus? Admetus? Idas?

"Open your eyes, Jason!" There was no mistaking that tone. Acastus!

He forced his eyes to open, and now the light was growing stronger, spilling over him, warming him. Flames, a campfire. He tried to sit up, and immediately pain and nausea overwhelmed him.

A hand on his shoulder. "Steady, Jason. You've taken a bad hit."

He touched his fingertips to where the pain was worst and found that a bandage had been wrapped around his head.

"It's as clean as I could make it," said Alcestis, "and I found some agrimony growing nearby. I ground it with a rock and used it to treat the wound."

"You can stop fussing over him now," said Acastus. "He's going to be fine."

"What happened?" Jason's voice was a dry rasp. "I thought I was dead."

"You almost were," said Lynceus. "Luckily Idas just had time to reach down and grab you before the current carried us off."

Jason was sitting upright now, still dizzy. Idas passed him a water skin, and he drank thirstily.

"I'm surprised you didn't have your fill of water when you went under," Idas joked.

"Thanks—thanks to you I didn't." Jason's voice was still raspy.

Idas shrugged. "We'd all have gone under if we'd hit that rock, but you managed to turn us just enough to keep the boat safe."

Jason blinked and looked around him. Things were still spinning. "Where are we?"

"Soon after we got you back aboard, things started to calm down on the river, " said Acastus. "By nightfall we'd managed to reach the northern shore of Lake Boebis, so we stopped here to make camp."

"Rather than risk getting lost," Admetus added.

"We need to get moving again," Jason said. He stood up, only to find the earth swaying.

Idas jumped up and helped him sit down again. "Easy, easy, you're no use to us in this condition."

Reluctantly Jason agreed. He drank a bit more of

the water and, after a while, even ate some of the bread that Alcestis had crumbled and made into a paste. Only then did he feel better.

"We'll grab a few hours' sleep and start up again before dawn," Acastus said.

Even a few hours made a difference to them all, though Lynceus insisted that Jason take the stern seat for the rest of the trip. During their brief stopover, Idas had cut down a sapling to replace the broken oar.

The fresh air gusting up from the lake helped to clear Jason's head as they moved swiftly over the calm water. They spotted several fishing boats out for an early catch, and the fishermen waved to them as they sped past.

There was a village on the far side, and as soon as they had dragged the *Swift* ashore, Acastus called together some of the locals.

"I am your prince, Acastus, son of Pelias," he announced to them, "and I need your help."

"He's the prince, sure enough," one old farmer told his friends. "I saw him last year, standing beside his father when those bandits were being condemned to death."

"Has anybody here seen any sign of centaurs?" Acastus asked.

A murmur went through the little crowd, and a man stepped forward. "I was out in my boat about twilight," he said, "off the western shore of the lake. I heard the noise of horses' hooves, and I looked out for chariots. Instead I saw a couple of centaurs, though it sounded like more. They disappeared into the trees, and I saw no more of them."

"They're here!" cried Jason. "Assuming they stopped for the night, we may just have got here in time."

"Is there a wagon around here?" Acastus demanded.

"Laentes has one," somebody called out.

"But you'd be as quick pulling it yourself as trusting that old nag of his!" another said with a laugh.

"Someone fetch this Laentes," Acastus commanded. "We have to get to the city as fast as possible."

"The rest of you need to go on to Iolcus," said Jason. "I'll try to find out where the centaurs have gone."

Acastus shot him a sharp look, but there was understanding in his eyes.

"What? In your condition? And alone? You can't be serious, Jason," Admetus said.

"I'm fine now," Jason assured him quietly. "Chiron told me to recover the Gorgon's blood, to keep it from being used. That's what I have to do." He didn't dare tell them that he'd no intention of entrusting himself to King Pelias' protection. Once he was in Pelias' court, the story of his birth would be revealed and his life would be forfeit. More than that, Chiron had made it clear that under no conditions should King Pelias have the Gorgon's blood.

"Look," he added, "what good is it for all of us to go

to Iolcus? King Pelias has an army. He doesn't need us. We don't even know yet where the centaurs are, or what their plan is. Somebody has to track them down."

Jason took a swallow from his water skin and wiped his brow.

"Won't they just be going straight to Iolcus?" Lynceus asked.

Acastus gave a short snort. "There aren't enough of them to take a whole city," he said slowly while Jason nodded. "Not a city like Iolcus."

"Don't forget the poison," said Jason.

"No one is forgetting the poison," Acastus retorted. "I was just pointing out—"

"How could they use the poison in battle?" Idas asked.

Lynceus said quickly, "Poison their arrows?"

"I don't remember seeing any bows at Mount Ossa," said Jason.

"Or arrows," Acastus added. "And we were a lot closer than you two."

"They might have *hidden* the bows and arrows someplace," said Lynceus.

"Even poison arrows wouldn't make a decisive difference in a battle," said Jason.

Acastus agreed. "My father's warriors outnumber them four to one."

"And the centaurs know it," Jason said slowly. "Which means it's not a *battle* they're looking for. At least not until after the poison's done its work."

"What work?" Idas exclaimed in exasperation. "You can't just throw the jar at your enemy. And if the wind shifts—"

"They could ride into the city," mused Alcestis, "pretending friendship, have dinner with my father and all the nobles, and poison the wine. That way—"

"They're not exactly built for stealth," Admetus pointed out. "And not bright enough to pretend a friendship. Even if your father would let them in the gates."

Idas smacked a fist against his thigh. "For all the ideas we've come up with, we might as well all have drowned in the river!"

His words jolted Jason's mind back to the rapids. For a moment he'd believed he was going with Charon across the Styx, the poisonous river that wound its way seven times around the Land of the Dead.

"Poisonous river," he murmured.

Acastus' eyes narrowed. "What?"

"They're going to poison the water!" Jason cried. "Nothing could be faster. Or more deadly."

"Of course!" Acastus looked grim.

Jason turned to him. "What's the most important water source for Iolcus?"

Without hesitation Acastus answered, "The spring of Melokrene to the northwest of the city. It flows into a pool called the Pool of Demeter." His eyes were wide. "From there it feeds into every underground stream and well for miles. Every year our priests offer sacrifices there to purify the water."

Jason leaned forward, put his hand on Acastus' shoulder. "That's it! From that one place the Gorgon's blood could spread throughout the whole country. Demeter's Pool. Hundreds would die before they realized the danger."

"And if the water's poisoned, it would seep into the land," added Admetus.

"Crops would fail," said Alcestis in a stricken voice. "Our herds would die, too."

"Wait a moment, wait a moment," Idas said. "No poison could do all that."

"No *ordinary* poison could," said Jason, "but the blood of the Gorgon Medusa is deadlier than anyone can imagine."

Acastus jumped up. "We have to go straight to the spring," he said. "It shouldn't take us more than a couple of hours to get there from here. Alcestis can take the wagon to Iolcus and warn Father."

"It looks like the five of us have a bit farther to go yet," said Admetus with a weary grin.

"Admetus, I want you to go to the city with Alcestis," Acastus said.

"Me? Why me?"

Acastus laid a hand on his cousin's arm. "Because I need someone I can trust to protect her. There's no telling what dangers may still lie between here and the city."

Admetus glanced at Alcestis and gave a nod. There was a flush to his cheeks.

"And I need someone my father will listen to," Acastus added. "Tell him to arm his men and prepare his chariots."

"You can trust me, cousin," Admetus said.

"But I have as much right to find the centaurs as any of you," Alcestis said.

Jason moved smoothly to her side. "If your father isn't warned, none of what we do matters here. You have the more difficult task. If you don't make it through . . ."

She nodded. "All right, Jason. But I don't see why I need a companion."

He said carefully, "If one of you doesn't get through, there's hope the other can."

"Ah." She seemed happy with that explanation.

By now the wagon had appeared. Alcestis and Admetus climbed up beside Laentes the farmer and set off on the track to Iolcus.

"If we're right, we'll find the centaurs at the pool of Demeter," said Jason.

"And what do we do then?" Lynceus asked warily. "There are only four of us now."

"Do whatever we can to delay them until my father catches up with us," said Acastus

"And get that jar of poison!" Jason added.

CHAPTER TWENTY-FIVE

THE TRAIL

The villagers provided the boys with fresh supplies of water and food and wished them well on their journey. As they set off, Jason was grimly silent. He knew that whenever King Pelias appeared, it would mean the end of his fragile alliance with Acastus.

He had faced so many dangers already, and yet one of his own companions was still the deadliest threat of all.

By midday they had reached a group of rocks, like the building stones of giants, piled one atop the other. They decided to take a break and rest for a few minutes in the shade.

Lynceus clambered to the top of the highest boulder

and, shielding his eyes from the sun, scanned the surrounding countryside. "I can't see anything but more hills and more trees."

"But we are within an hour of Demeter's Pool," Acastus proclaimed. "I know this place. I have camped here with Father. Take heart. It is not long now."

Jason was surprised at Acastus' speech. It was the first time he'd sounded like a leader.

The boys responded to his words. A new sense of purpose lent them all strength. They stood and went forward and, though little was said over the next several miles, there was energy in their walking.

When at last they spotted the gleam of water through the trees below them, Acastus—who had been brooding the whole way—spoke up.

"Lynceus, you and Idas get up to the top of that hill over there!" he commanded, pointing to a small hillock on the top of which was a white marble shrine. "See if there's any sign of the centaurs. Jason and I will keep going on toward the lake."

The two brothers followed his orders at once.

Acastus strode off quickly through the light foliage so that Jason had to hurry to catch up.

"There's something else on your mind, isn't there?"

"Of course there is," Acastus replied abruptly. "Hasn't it crossed *your* mind that the centaurs may already have come and gone? The water may already be carrying its poison to my city."

"You're right," Jason admitted.

"And there's only one way to find out for certain," Acastus said grimly.

"You're going to drink the water!" Jason exclaimed.

"Do you have a better plan? We don't have any time to waste. If the water's safe, we'll know the centaurs haven't arrived yet. If not, you will have to make sure that the news of the danger is spread as quickly as possible. Thousands of lives will be at stake."

"You may be right," Jason admitted hesitantly, "but there's no reason the drinker has to be you."

"There's *every* reason!" Acastus increased his pace. "*I* am the prince of Iolcus!"

Jason matched him step for step. "That's no reason to kill yourself. After all, *I'm* the one Chiron charged with bringing back the Gorgon's blood. It's my fault we didn't get it."

Acastus rounded on him, his face twisted with anger and pain. "Back at Mount Ossa, I almost had the poisoned blood in my hands," he said, his voice tight and strained, "but I missed my chance. If this land is to die because of *my* failure, then I should die with it." He turned back to the path and rounded a final turning.

There ahead lay the Pool of Demeter, shaped like a silver shield.

Jason grabbed for Acastus, but at his touch, Acastus rounded on him and whipped out his sword.

Without thinking, Jason leaped back and drew his

own sword, his hand trembling with shock.

"I told you it would come to this, Jason," said Acastus. There was a quiver in his voice that he was trying hard to control. "I told you we'd settle matters with swords, warrior to warrior."

Jason could feel the pulse pounding in his temple, the sun beating hot on his face. Both Gorgon's blood jars lost, the prince of Iolcus dead—could he go back to Chiron with news like that?

"No, Acastus. If Chiron were here, he'd take the test himself, and I must serve in his place."

Rage flared in Acastus' eyes. "Why? Because you think that you are the true prince of Iolcus and not I?"

He lashed out with his sword, but Jason blocked the blow. The bronze blades clanged together, the sound echoing through the trees.

"That's got nothing—"

Before Jason could finish, Acastus struck again. And again. With each new blow Jason was driven farther back up the path.

Acastus paused, his face red, his chest heaving. "Don't you see that this is your chance, Jason? If I drink the poisoned water, then you will be prince of Iolcus. It will be a blighted land filled with withered crops and dead cattle, but still you will be its prince."

"Is that what you're so afraid of?" Jason asked. "Can't you see how much your people will need you if the worst happens? How much your father will need you?"

"You know nothing of kings, Jason!" Acastus yelled. "I would be a shame to my people, a weakling. No one could rule that way." He attacked again, bronze ringing on bronze. One blow, two, then a third.

For a moment, they paused again, both boys exhausted and sweating.

"You can't beat me with a sword, Jason," Acastus said, gulping air. "I've trained an hour each day with my father's royal guards since I was six years old."

"Then why are you so out of breath, mighty prince?" asked Jason, though he, too, was gasping.

Acastus slashed at him.

As Jason stepped back to avoid the blow, his foot slipped on damp leaves. He stumbled to his knees, shoving the edge of his blade up before his face. The impact of blade on blade jarred the sword from Jason's fingers, and it fell onto the ground.

Looking up, Jason saw the prince looming over him, poised for a killing thrust.

In the back of his mind, Jason heard Hera's laughter.

CHAPTER TWENTY-SIX

THE SPRING

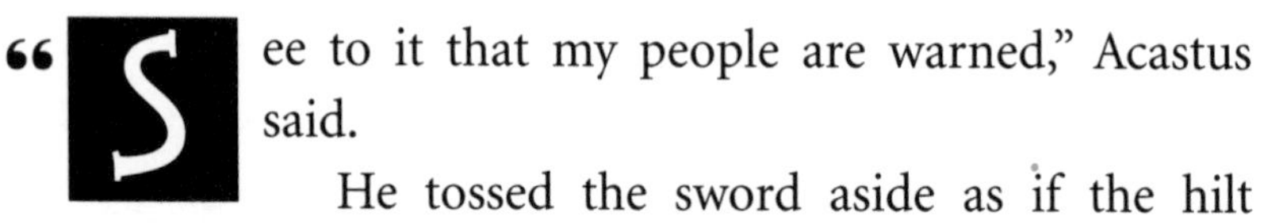

“See to it that my people are warned,” Acastus said.

He tossed the sword aside as if the hilt burned his fingers, then turned and ran toward the pool.

Jason jumped up. “You may be better with a sword,” he muttered, “but I’m the faster runner.” He raced off in pursuit, and—at the last second—Jason threw himself at Acastus, wrapping his arms tightly around the other boy’s legs.

Acastus toppled to the ground, and they rolled together in a flurry of kicks and punches.

“The gods damn you, Jason!” Acastus cried. “Do you *want* to die?” He jammed a knee into Jason’s belly and made a grab for his throat.

Jason shifted his weight and flipped the prince onto his back, pinning his shoulders to the ground.

"No more than you, *Prince* Acastus." He was panting. There was a sharp pain under his breastbone. His arms ached. "But if you want a witness to your sacrifice, you should have picked somebody more obliging."

Clenching his fist, he smacked Acastus across the jaw, hard enough to leave him stunned. Pushing himself up, he staggered the last few yards to the lake and dropped to his knees.

To his right several sparkling streams were pouring down a series of high, rocky tiers to splash into the pool. The water looked pure and clear.

Innocent, he thought. But he knew that if the Gorgon's blood had already been poured in, the running waters would have long since diluted its crimson color. Yet it would still be just as deadly.

Jason had not been raised as the prince of Iolcus, but he had been raised with a sense of duty. It was clear to him that his duty was to protect the land and its people just as a shepherd protects his flock—even at the risk of his life. Taking a deep breath, aware that it might be his last, he cupped his hands and dipped them into the pool. He lifted the water to his lips and swallowed. As he did so he was aware of a sudden splash to his right.

Acastus had caught up, thrown himself flat on the bank, and plunged his head into the pool. He came up, choking on the water he had swallowed, his face dripping.

Coughing three times, he rolled onto his back.

"So now we die together, eh?"

"Or live," said Jason. The water had tasted normal, but what did *normal* mean? Each beat of his heart seemed to measure out a vast distance of time, like the slow boom of a far-off tide.

One beat.

Two.

Acastus sat up. The boys looked at each other.

Three . . . four . . .

"Are we dead yet?" Acastus asked.

Jason squinted about him. "The sun's too bright and the grass too green for this to be Hades' realm." He sighed. "I think . . . we're alive."

"That's good news," Acastus declared. All at once he began to chuckle. Then he threw back his head and laughed long and loud.

Jason flopped onto his back and dissolved into laughter as well. It sounded rich, foolish, and wonderful.

Eventually they calmed down and remembered why they were here and how much they still had to do.

Just then, Lynceus and Idas came charging through the bushes. "Dust," Lynceus gasped. "To the southeast."

"Great clouds of it," Idas confirmed. "Could be horses."

"It's coming from the direction of the city," said Acastus. "The centaurs wouldn't be coming that way."

"So it must be—" Lynceus began.

"Chariots!" Idas finished for him.

Acastus nodded. "Warriors from Iolcus," said Acastus. He turned to Jason. "My father's horses are the swiftest in Thessaly."

"We still can't wait around for him," said Jason. "We have to guard the spring."

"You'll need these," said Idas, tossing their swords at their feet. "I found them lying on the ground. Is there any point asking what's been going on?"

"We were having a race," Acastus replied. He snatched up his sword and sheathed it. "Lynceus, go and meet the chariots. Tell them where we are and that they need to hurry."

"Won't you need another sword at your side?" Lynceus asked.

"We need reinforcements even more," said Idas, clapping him on the back. "Go, fetch them."

Lynceus gave his brother a stern look. "You take care of yourself till I get back," he warned, wagging his finger at him.

As Lynceus ran off through the trees, Jason retrieved his own sword and the three boys started up the stony slope, working their way around the shoulder of the crag. They peered down through the rocks and beheld an awesome sight.

On the plain below, the centaurs were approaching from the north. They were waving clubs over their heads, whooping and yelling.

Jason jerked back and signaled the others to keep low.

Below them, the centaur host had come to a halt. They formed a broad crescent around Kentauros and let out a ragged cheer. Wedged under Kentauros' muscular arm Jason could see the red jar containing the Gorgon's blood.

"There may be hundreds of them," Acastus said, "but no more than two or three of them at a time can climb up here to the spring. That evens the odds a bit."

"Maybe long enough for Lynceus to bring up your father's troops. . . ." Idas said. But the three looked at one another, all thinking the same thing.

"Only if we can get our hands on that jar," Jason said at last.

"The important thing is to keep the spring safe," said Acastus, "even at the cost of our lives."

Just then they heard Kentauros bellow, "My brothers, now we shall have our vengeance. Ages ago we were driven from this land by the hordes of man. Now we shall turn this stolen country into a wasteland. The survivors will become our slaves and our prey! Onward . . . on to the source of Demeter's Pool."

A huge cheer went up. The centaurs drummed their hooves on the ground and chanted, "KEN-TAU-ROS! KEN-TAU-ROS!"

"We need a place for an ambush," said Idas. "Surprise is the only advantage we'll have."

They climbed up the slope, scrambling over rocks to where the spring gushed out of a hole in the crag before splitting into several lesser streams on its way down. They found a stony outcropping where, crouched in the shadows, they waited.

Jason drew his sword and ran his thumb lightly over the edge to assure himself of its sharpness.

"What do you think old Chiron would say if he could see us now?" Idas asked.

"He'd probably say we'd come poorly equipped," said Acastus, "that we should have planned better."

"No," said Jason, "I think he'd be proud, proud of all of us for making it this far together." He stretched his sword out before him and the others laid their blades on top of it.

"We are bound together now," said Jason, "sworn comrades in the battle to come."

"Comrades," said Idas, voice harsh.

"Comrades," said Acastus, his face suddenly serene.

Now there were hoofbeats approaching from below. Jason peeked around the rock and saw Kentauros coming up the slope with Nessus right behind him. Kentauros looked bigger than ever, his skin even paler in the sunlight than in the cave. It was pulled so tight, his bones were visible beneath it, as if he were still partly dead.

Kentauros paused and turned to face his followers, who had spread out below, surrounding the pool. He raised the jar of Gorgon's blood above his head, and a cheer went up that chilled Jason to the bone.

"Idas, can you distract Nessus?" he asked.

Idas grinned. "I'll try to do more than that."

"Acastus, you and I will tackle Kentauros."

"You go after the jar," said Acastus. "I'll try to kill Kentauros. Let's pray one of us succeeds."

Meanwhile, Kentauros had trotted up to the spring, pausing there as if to savor his moment of cruel satisfaction. His grin was a skeleton's. He was about to pull the stopper from the jar when the three boys jumped from their hiding place and came skidding down the rocky slope, yelling a war cry.

CHAPTER TWENTY-SEVEN

BLOOD AND WATER

castus charged the huge centaur with his sword, screaming curses as he ran.

At the same time, Jason leaped off the slope, landing on Kentauros' horse back. But he had overshot his mark and began to slip off the other side. Frantically he hooked his left arm around the centaur's waist, where the two parts of the body joined together.

From the corner of his eye Jason saw Idas ducking—barely in time to keep Nessus' club from smashing his skull like an eggshell. As Idas pressed forward, he cut a gash in the centaur's foreleg.

Just then Kentauros reared up, pounding his hooves at Acastus like a pair of hammers. Jason felt himself falling off, and he made a desperate grab for the centaur's shaggy mane. Twisting his fingers in the thick, tangled hair, he hung on as Kentauros bucked and kicked.

Jason tried to make a clean thrust at the centaur with his sword, but his blade slid over Kentauros' shoulder, only scoring a deep groove in the white flesh. To his amazement, not a single drop of blood sprang from the wound.

"No more of your fleabites!" Kentauros snarled, and reached back, clamping bony fingers around Jason's throat and hoisting him up. Trained in wrestling, Jason knew that if he tried to resist his opponent's strength, his neck might snap. He went slack, and Kentauros flung him to the ground, where he rolled with the impact until he slammed against a tree. His sword, shaken loose from his fingers, went clattering down the rocks to land with a splash in the pool far below.

Meanwhile, bruised and bloodied, Acastus had bravely renewed his attack. He lunged at the giant centaur and was able to bury his sword up to the hilt in the pale flesh of Kentauros' belly. Bellowing his rage, Kentauros swatted the boy aside like a fly.

Acastus fell into the shallow stream and lay there, stunned.

"I didn't return from the dead to die again so soon!" Kentauros roared. He gripped the sword hilt in one hand and pulled the blade from his body as easily as he would have plucked out a troublesome splinter. Again there was no blood, just a glaring purple bruise around the ugly wound.

Jason realized that Kentauros had been dead for so long, the Gorgon's blood could not restore him to true life, only to a semblance of it. Though Kentauros moved and spoke, he was no more a living creature than an effigy formed of wax and straw.

Then how can he be killed? Jason thought.

Sure of his triumph, Kentauros tore the stopper from the clay jar. "Do you see, Lapithes?" he cried, taunting his long-dead enemy in his booming voice. "Can you see me from your place in the Land of the Dead? I bring misery and doom to your descendants! I will have my vengeance at last!"

He was poised to pour the Gorgon's blood into the water, right over the spot where Acastus lay. Acastus turned, groaned, and tried to rise, but it was too late. Jason knew the prince could not get up in time.

Putting a hand on his own sword belt, Jason suddenly felt—Lynceus' sling! That might give him a chance—the smallest chance imaginable, but it was all he had. Quickly he snatched the sling up, found a stone in the leather pouch, and fitted it into place. There was time for only one shot.

Kentauros had already raised the deadly jar high above his head. In another instant he would pour the blood into the water where Acastus lay, bringing death to the land of Iolcus.

Jason fixed his eyes on his target and whirled the sling so hard, he felt his wrist might snap.

"If any gods are watching over us, may they guide my hand now," he prayed.

He released the stone, and it shot through the air, striking the jar like the blow of a chisel. The jar shattered, and the Gorgon's blood burst forth, drenching Kentauros, soaking into his ghastly flesh as though he were an immense sponge. In an instant, the giant centaur's bones ignited like dry kindling, making a bonfire that consumed him in seconds. With a boom as loud as a thunderclap, he exploded in a blast of flame that shot straight up into the heavens.

For an instant the whole landscape was bathed in a crimson glow, as if drenched in blood. Then it faded, and all that was left of the monstrous centaur was a scattering of white ash blowing about on the breeze.

Nessus stumbled back in shock, and below, a groan of horror and despair rose up from the rest of the centaurs.

Then there came a very different sound, a defiant battle cry from hundreds of human throats. Jason looked down and saw that King Pelias had arrived with his army.

A line of chariots, spread out in attack formation, was already sweeping around the shore of the pool toward the centaurs. Arrows and javelins flew through the air. Then the armored warriors, in perfect synchronization, dismounted and advanced on foot with their long spears and towerlike shields held before them.

After seeing their leader annihilated as if by the wrath of the gods, the centaurs had no heart left for fighting. They turned like a herd of frightened horses, galloping off to the north. Nessus managed to scramble down the slope in time to join his brothers in their desperate and unruly retreat.

Idas helped Acastus to his feet, and the two of them gave a cheer. Jason wanted to cry out, too, but his ribs were too sore.

The charioteers pursued the centaurs for a short while, killing a few and wounding many more. But soon the centaurs outran them, disappearing in the direction of their northern homeland.

At a blast from a great bronze trumpet, the king's troops were recalled.

By the time the boys had come down from the rocks, the chariots had been drawn into a rough circle. In the center stood King Pelias, acknowledging the cheers of his men with an upraised hand.

Lynceus, who'd been riding beside Pelias, ran to meet his friends, bombarding them with questions about the giant centaur, the jar of Gorgon's blood, and whether any of the blood had gotten into the water.

"Gone, all gone," was Jason's answer. He knew it was the truth.

Alcestis and Admetus came running from one of

the other chariots. The friends greeted one another eagerly.

Suddenly Pelias himself was looming over them, two guards standing on either side. Slowly he removed his golden helmet to reveal a tanned, battle-scarred face that was as hard and unyielding as his gilded armor. On his cheek was a purple mark, just as Jason had seen in the vision Hera had sent him. There was no mistaking the man.

Pelias' gray eyes seemed to bore right through the boys. "We were just in time to see that beacon you lit," he said. "You looked to be severely outnumbered."

"That was no bonfire, Father," Acastus said. "That was Kentauros, the leader of the centaurs. The poisoned blood he planned to pour into the spring destroyed him instead."

Jason looked from father to son, and he could see the resemblance clearly, though it was less than it would have been a week ago. Acastus no longer carried himself with arrogance, nor did he speak as if his every word were a royal decree. Jason doubted King Pelias would have risked his own life drinking from the pool as his son had done. He would have ordered one of his men to do it in his place. Of that Jason was sure.

Acastus gave his father a brief account of their journey from Lake Boebis, carefully leaving out any mention of Jason.

"I've already met Admetus and Lynceus," said the king, "and now you have told me of this brave warrior Idas, but who is this other youth?"

He fixed his hawklike gaze on Jason.

Jason knew that if King Pelias spotted a resemblance between himself and his father, Aeson, it could be the end of both of them. He bowed his head, like a servant humbled in the presence of his lord.

"He's an orphan," Acastus replied quickly, "a servant of Chiron. He acted as our guide. That's all."

The other boys looked surprised, and even angry at that, and Admetus started to say something. But Jason shook his head, to let them know that this was what he wanted.

Pelias immediately lost interest in Jason and turned to his troops. "Board your chariots, my warriors!" he commanded. "Let us return to Iolcus and celebrate this victory with feasting and song! Let us praise the name of Prince Acastus, a son of whom any man would be proud!"

"Acastus!" the warriors cheered, drumming the butts of their spears on the ground.

"My companions should be honored," said Acastus, motioning to them with his hand, "and my sister, too."

"Of course they are invited to the feast," said the king. "And what about your guide?"

Acastus shuffled his feet uneasily. "We don't need

him anymore. He should go back to Chiron at once and tell him what's happened."

"I'll have one of my charioteers take him as far as the mountains," said Pelias. He turned and walked off, duty done.

Acastus took Jason aside. "One day your part in this will be honored," he said, "but right now it would be dangerous for you to attract too much attention from my father."

"Thank you, Acastus," said Jason, and meant it. He smiled. "Then you've changed your mind about us settling things like warriors?"

"We *have* settled things like warriors," Acastus replied, "fighting side by side. How you stayed on that creature's back I'll never know! And the way you fired that stone!"

Jason laughed. "There was more luck to that shot than I care to admit, Acastus."

"What matters," Acastus said, "is that you never stopped fighting. From now on we are comrades in arms, whatever happens in the future."

For a moment Jason could not think what to say. He wondered if Hera had guided his shot or if she'd abandoned him to his fate long before. Either way, with Acastus offering himself as a friend, Jason knew he could never help the goddess in her scheme for revenge. If ever he returned to Iolcus, it would not be with an army, but alone and unarmed.

"I can't guess what the future holds for us, Acastus," he told the prince, "but I promise you this: If ever I come for my throne, I will do no harm either to you or your father."

"And I promise no harm will come to you, either. Let the gods decide the rest." Acastus put a hand on Jason's shoulder.

"In the meantime," Jason said, "my mother and father are still living in Iolcus. . . ."

"You will find them safe and well when you come," Acastus promised. "I will see to it."

He offered his hand, and Jason clasped it firmly.

The other boys gathered around them.

"I can't pretend to understand what's going on, Jason," said Admetus, "but I suppose if you don't want anyone to know about your part in all of this, we'll go along with that."

"Thank you," said Jason. "One day everything will be made clear."

"When that day comes, Jason," said Lynceus, "if you should need a sharp pair of eyes—"

"Or a strong arm," Idas put in.

They spoke together, "Just send for us."

"Me, too," said Admetus. "If you should ever need somebody who can . . . well, somebody who's willing to help, I will come."

"I will remember all of you," Jason assured them. "And I hope that one day we will all travel together again."

"In that case I hope it's an easier journey than this one!" said Admetus.

"Easier?" Idas laughed. "Why, this was just a warm-up!"

And they all laughed with him, Jason the loudest of them all.

WHAT IS TRUE ABOUT THIS STORY?

Did the Heroic Age—the Age of Heroes—really exist?

Yes and no.

No—there was not a time when the gods took part in human battles, nor were there harpies flying about mountaintops or centaurs galloping along the plains. There were no Gorgons, monsters whose blood could bring both life and death.

But yes—there was once a rich and powerful civilization in Greece that we call Mycenaean, where each city was a separate state with its own king but where the people were united by a single language. One of these was the kingdom of Thessaly, on the plains, where King Jason eventually reigned.

In the old mythological stories, Aeson—then rightful king of Iolcus—gave up his throne to his half brother, Pelias. Fearing his own baby son Jason would be killed by the greedy new king, Aeson sent the infant to the mountains to be reared by Chiron, the wise centaur.

When Jason was grown, he came down out of the mountains to demand the crown from Pelias. Pelias had been warned by an oracle to beware of a one-sandaled lad, and since Jason arrived wearing only one sandal, Pelias knew he had to destroy the young man. He suggested that before becoming king, Jason should first go on a perilous quest to retrieve the Golden Fleece, which rightfully belonged in Thessaly. Pelias did not expect Jason to return.

Jason was thrilled to go on such a quest. He rounded up fifty of the heroes of Greece—including the king's son, Acastus; Lynceus (whose eyesight was so keen he reputedly could see right through the earth) and his brother, Idas; Admetus; Hercules; Theseus; Orpheus; Nestor and (in some versions of the story) the female hero Atalanta. Many are the names in the folklore, as Greek families added to the story for centuries in order to claim an ancestor who sailed with Jason.

Jason's boat was built by an innovative builder named Argos and was named the *Argo* after him. The fifty who sailed on her were known as the Argonauts. Some folklorists feel that this adventure may have—

in part—been based on one of the earliest maritime expeditions known to Western civilization.

The love story of Admetus and Alcestis is told in mythology, and thence in a play by Euripides based on the folklore. Admetus was another king in mythic Thessaly. The god Apollo, learning that Admetus was destined to an early death, conned the Fates (with the help of a great deal of wine) into granting Admetus a longer life if someone would die in his place. His father and mother refused, but his wife, Alcestis, agreed to offer herself. Coming to visit his friend Admetus, Hercules learned of what had happened. He intercepted Thanatos—the messenger of death—and wrestled him into submission, freeing Alcestis. And so the loving couple were reunited. This myth gives no reason for Admetus' early death, but we have provided one in our story, for herein Admetus brings down a curse on himself by using the Gorgon's blood to restore Alcestis to life.

The story of Melampus and the little serpents who licked his ears and thus gave him the ability to hear animals speak also comes from Greek mythological tradition.

The centaurs (in Greek they are called Kentauroi), half human and half horse, also were supposed to dwell in Thessaly, on and around Mount Pelion. They all had a bad reputation, especially Nessus, who tried to steal away Hercules' wife and was killed for it. Chiron was a different kind of centaur, the son of a god who had sired him when in horse shape. He was known to be both wise and just, learned in both music and medicine. The stories say he educated many of the Greek heroes, including Asclepius, Jason, and Achilles.

Alcestis' prayers to Hera and to the god of the river are both adapted from several found in a collection of prayers.

Stories. Legends. Tales.

But a young man—even a mythic hero—must have a childhood and adolescence that foretell his future deeds. We know little about Jason's childhood from the tales except that he was taught by Chiron. We know from the stories of his famous expedition on board the *Argo* that he was easily persuaded to go on a dangerous mission; that he was heroic, ambitious, brave, headstrong, willing to put his body on the line for his friends, and considered a great leader.

We have taken the Jason of the legends and tales and projected him backward into his adolescence, using what archeologists have told us about the civilization he would have inhabited if he had been a real young man.

Or a young hero.